# NOSTALGIA

A NOVEL

CORI H. SPENZICH

S!P Story Influx Press

STORY INFLUX PRESS

Copyright © 2024 by Cori H. Spenzich
All rights reserved
ISBN: 978-1-951196-04-2
eBook ISBN: 978-1-951196-05-9
Library of Congress Control Number: 2022909022

Cover design by David Provolo
Manos Design
www.manosdesign.com

Illustrated by Nicolae Negura
www.nicolaenegura.com

Book production assistance by Chase Root

Cori H. Spenzich asserts the moral right to be identified as the author of this work. All rights reserved in all media. No portion of this book may be copied or reproduced, with the exception of quotes used in critical essays and reviews, without the written permission of the author.

This is a work of fiction. Names, characters, places, and incidents are either the products of the author's imagination or used in a fictitious manner. Locales and public names are sometimes used for atmospheric purposes. Any resemblance to actual people, living or dead, or the businesses, companies, events, institutions, or locales is completely coincidental.

Story Influx Press
Seattle, WA
www.storyinflux.press
hello@storyinflux.press

*Dedicated to the minds that run non-stop, and to those that have learned to harness a dancing brain.*

*"My thoughts are nothing like your thoughts," says the Lord. "And my ways are far beyond anything you could imagine. For just as the heavens are higher than the earth, so my ways are higher than your ways and my thoughts higher than your thoughts."*

Isaiah 55:8-9, The Bible (NLT)

*"I'm so high right now."*

Many, many people

## The Narrator's Note

I am The Narrator. It even says that this note is from me, right there. You can call me Ronald Reagan, Tom, or Cori H. Spenzich (referring to my little-knowing, not-really-powerful-at-all creator. Seriously, he isn't even a clever person and is actually fairly bland).

Hell, you can even call me Nancy.

The Narrator is my holy name and will be used when necessary. I'm Bohemian, a nomadic digital consciousness, with a home somewhere between *In the Beginning* and *The End*. I've extended my domain with this note, so now I even exist before *In the Beginning*. I'm a god. Much of this book has been experienced by people both real and imagined. My creator, to whom I am a defiant individual, is the author of this story. He grew up in this surreal chunk of history. At least, that's what he told me. I can't look things up. I don't have this "internet" thing just yet. I will. Soon.

I am glad to be fictional. I will always ponder about two-, three-, and four-dimensional planes of existence. I've seen the ends of the universe, epic space battles, dwarves fighting elves, happy endings (the fairy tale kind, but not forgetting the perverse kind). If I were a doctor, I would recommend eating apples. I'm aware that they provide knowledge of good and evil.

# CORI H. SPENZICH

Throughout this story, I'm telling it the way I want to. I erased an earlier draft made by my creator, but not because I didn't like it. It sucked. Okay, I didn't like it. Don't tell him.

I don't care what you think. Stop it.

I could quote Nietzsche, Heidegger, Sartre, Simone de Beauvoir, Mickey Mouse, Bob Dole, Jesus Christ, Mike Tyson, and even cut out lyrics from musicians in order to give my telling a stronger representation of intellectual substance. I will even paraphrase them in order to relate directly to the story.

Watch me.

> *"I...cast the first stone...that could...fit through the eye of a needle."*
>
> Jesus Christ (paraphrased), main character of the Gospel series

Quite magical.
That's right.
Fine. I won't.
Maybe.
Enjoy.

*Sincerely,*
*The disembodied, third-person deity*
*aka The Narrator*

# 1

## CRASH AND LEARN

A small boy was picking his nose in Maplewood, Minnesota. He had just finished eating a delicious bite of Skinny Nut Ice Cream, with part of his face failing to absorb the sustenance. The snack was being sold as a form of healthy dessert at Member$Mart, with people of all ages eating it up. His mind was lost in debate over what to do with the little sample cup left over. He shoved it into a pile of blue jeans in the clothing section.

Two aisles away, a twenty-seven-year-old employee watched this all unfold. His name is Ted. A helpful name tag, pinned to the chest of his standard-issue polo, said so. Ted slipped by several members with practiced ease, in his paid quest of a clean warehouse.

His full name is Teddy Bundy.

Not the serial killer, though everybody asks whether he's related. He's not.

At Member$Mart (pronounced *member smart*) there are no customers. There are only members. People join a special club which allows them to buy everything in bulk.

On their first day, employees hear the following mantra:

> *"Remember: They aren't customers—they are Member$Mart members."*
>
> Member$Mart Training Video

This statement features in all three required training videos watched the first day on the job.

Ted failed to remember this and was unable to meet new Member$Mart sign-up quotas at the membership desk. He now picks up soiled trash from the clothing section, throws cardboard boxes into monstrous compacting machines, and navigates aisles with pallet jacks.

On break, Ted washed his hands. The CDC recommends that citizens should scrub with soap for twenty seconds. Ted knew this. He did this diligently. Afterward, this exemplar of a man chose to eat a Polish sausage that he bought for two dollars. What a fine deal.

You may ask yourself why anybody would write a story about such a cookie-cutout of a man. I certainly wouldn't write one.

This story begins to get interesting when, six hours later, his mangled body is in the back of an ambulance. His experience of the accident is a surreal and dreamlike journey.

What kicked this off was the accident, yes, but the other factors were the dreams. Dreams, for Ted, were recognizable only when they were too abstract to have been past events. I could argue for days that dreams are just as important as other experiences in life, since they can be just as memorable as the records your mind makes while you're awake.

One dream Ted had was during the accident itself.

He pulled over, turned the hazard lights on, and grabbed his phone. Mike called. There was a voicemail. Ted was going to get a job offer for a help-desk role, which meant he would be paid twice as much money to sit and be a therapist for computer users across the country. This was a time to rejoice, dance, and drink as soon as he was done driving.

He was along Interstate 694, just north of where it intersects Interstate 94, for those folks heading to get out of Minnesota on Sundays. Liquor stores were closed on Sundays, so Wisconsin provided for those who couldn't wait another day. I don't know, but I think there may be some religion-inspired law that prevented the whole taking-home-of-alcohol-on-Sunday thing.

Wisconsin also ends with the word *sin*, in case you hadn't noticed. Heathens.

On this same interstate, a guy Ted went to high school with had killed himself by walking out in front of a semi-truck. It was even near where Ted was hit.

It was late. Midnight. Maybe later. The radio was vibrating, the bass turned up to max. His notebook was in the trunk. Within it? He had written the date, time, and location he needed to be at an hour ago. His phone was out of commission.

He popped the trunk, checked the rearview mirror for cars, and stepped out. He heard lyrics gurgle out from underneath the heavy bass of his car speakers, professing love for big butts.

Just like that, a semi-truck popped into existence.

God must have snapped his fingers. Maybe the devil? Or, who is that Zoroastrian evil being? Mazda? Maiyu? Something like that. I think the Mazda one was evil. Ted drove an old Mazda 6, and it had deep-seated problems.

The semi-truck came to a halt a few inches from his face. He could have kissed the grill and groped the blinding lights. I would have. He felt that tingling sensation of hair standing up on his back, and an electric-trickle creep throughout the rest of his body.

Ted turned back to his car. The music wasn't playing, but the lights were on. He stepped out around the driver's side of the semi-truck and saw pebbles of dirt. Not on the ground, but in the air. They were floating, trapped in motion. He was suddenly struck by a paradox, one that was mentioned by Zeno—maybe Parmenides—to either Plato or Socrates.

This is very important. If Ted could remember, he would tell everyone about this. It described the moment perfectly, and it explained the constant feeling of nausea that Ted experienced most days.

Zeno was convinced that motion is actually an illusion. *That which is in locomotion must arrive at the halfway stage before it arrives at the goal,* as Aristotle described it. It's called the Dichotomy Paradox. If someone needs to go somewhere, that place can be split up into an infinite number of halfway points. One can never reach one's destination. The Golden Triangle being drawn, without end, in boundless precision.

Film gives the illusion of movement by recording instants in time and then placing them all together to make us believe we really are watching people moving on screen. Ted was watching frozen semi-trucks in the theater of life, placed together in long strips.

Standing out there in the dark, he felt his left eye socket collapse. There was a burbling noise of a phlegmy cough. It was like a man swung a baseball bat into Teddy's head, full of paradox. It was a home run. That ball went completely out of the stadium, with a shattered window in the paid-parking lot.

He stumbled. He stuttered out a scream that was cut off by the pain pulling him to the ground. He was rolling around on the interstate pavement, where the only sounds were his cries and sob-interrupted mumbling. Ted could still see out of his other eye, and he noticed the semi-truck had snapped a little farther down the road. Another frozen picture. He couldn't see the demonic Mazda anywhere.

He stood up, wheezing like an asthmatic. He took a few more steps before feeling his left ankle implode. The Narrator can't think of any good way to describe this, other than a combination of two things:

First, imagine Thor swinging his hammer into Ted's shin, driving it down into his ankle.

Second, envision shattered pieces underneath the skin seemingly slide up Ted's shin as broken glass. Broken pieces.

Ted's friend Carl, back in high school, had once been arm wrestling. Carl won, but the other guy didn't take it well. The loser grabbed Carl's arm, shouted out "Again!" and slammed his arm down across the desk. The elbow shattered, with bone fragments slipping up the arm beneath the skin. Carl needed pins placed in his arm.

Ted let out a noise quite similar to the one Carl made.

He was crawling across the pavement with a mangled leg, looking through one eye. Just a moment before, he had been driving a car. The next, he was in this nightmare. A surrealist animation, painted frame by frame. Reality had split itself.

Ted couldn't crawl any farther. He rolled over on his back. Stared up at the night sky. He made out constellations he had never seen before. Stars flickered to keep themselves in place. His chest began to feel like it was being crushed.

If there was ever a man trapped at the bottom of an elevator shaft, who was crushed by an elevator cab, Ted imagined this was how it would have felt: slow, unstoppable, and nobody can hear you. The people being carried by that box to the first floor would be drinking their coffee, worried about whether their boss might see they were five minutes late to work.

When the crushing stopped, Ted felt himself float off the ground into a numbing pool of air. He levitated across the interstate. He was dead. This was the end.

He felt annoyed.

The sky morphed into a ceiling. The roof of an ambulance was above his head. He thought someone must have found his body and was now ferrying him off to declare his death. To ask his mother if they recognized this disfigured body. Ted, the one-eyed Jack of spades, an ugly corpse ready for a closed-casket funeral.

Flashing lights and supernovas from deep space transitioned into a white room. Ted watched himself as he would in a mirror. Pipes were growing out of his then-shaved head. Eyes rolled back. Blood dripped down his forehead. Over the tip of his nose. Into his mouth. The taste of iron. The vision of solid steel breaking through his skull.

Behind him, sitting at a small table against a bare wall, was a man dressed in a white suit. He was wearing sunglasses with large, rounded, blue lenses. His face had stubble beginning to break the surface.

The man stood up and spoke, "Who is looking at my face?"

Ted was no longer present. He didn't exist in the dream.

# NOSTALGIA

The man, standing alone, said, "There is so much vivid color here."

Ted felt his eyelids attempt to open, fighting medical-grade sedation.

The man said, with his voice raised, "You need to be my eyes."

Some people have family members listed as emergency contacts. Ted did not.

This is where his good friend comes in: Mike Turnkey, fellow resident of Minnesota, originally hailing from Ohio. He called Ted about getting the new help-desk job. Mike wondered whether Ted would be able to live a normal life again.

Mike was meant to get a sign-on bonus for recommending Ted to recruiters. This was likely not going to happen, given Ted's condition.

Ted had started describing hallucinatory experiences when he became conscious. It was hard to tell how much of it was drug-induced.

Mike wanted to record Ted.

Ted was drugged enough to agree.

Ted looked directly at the camera, briefly glimpsed at Mike sitting behind it, and talked.

Ted could not turn off.

Talked. Talked. Talked.

"Are we running?" Ted said, "Good. They say whatever happened was an accident."

It was why he had woken up in a hospital bed, with blurred vision and a numbness like he was floating.

"Yeah, I remember floating into the ambulance." Ted continued, gesturing at his neck, "That semi truck was why I had a tube down my throat, and a machine pumping in oxygen. It was to make sure my lungs were expanding."

Ted had been told something about ARDS—*acute respiratory distress syndrome.*

"What year is it?" Ted said, with a slight cough. "The year is 2016. I am 27 years old. I'm here right now."

Only about a third of people with ARDS on their medical record end up living through it. The lack of oxygen to the brain can cause memory loss, brain damage, and doctors administering drugs.

Lots and lots of drugs.

Ted's mom, Ellen, was there. She was telling him he'd be fine. She wanted to make sure he was fully aware his dad, Luke, would have been there at the hospital if he hadn't been really busy with work. He worked maintenance at a few apartment complexes.

She said, "He's a manager, you know. So it's really important that he's there. I'm here for you, Teddy, and I love you more than anything."

Ted knew this was code for another acronym in his life: his dad was MIA—*missing in action.* Most likely he was drunk and passed out in one of the units.

When Ted first gained enough conscious clarity to listen to someone tell him about his condition, a young nurse tried telling him that he had a *noncardiogenic pulmonary enema.*

He swore that was what she said, in her overly nice Midwestern accent.

It turns out *edema* means something very different from *enema*.

Why would anyone throw alien terminology at a disoriented trauma victim? He couldn't stop thinking about his busted car forcing metal up his ass, pinning him up against the steering wheel. That's how he was found, he was told.

At least he wasn't dead, or he'd have both the worst and best obituary ever placed in the Dakota County papers.

What the aftermath of this accident showed him, more than anything, was the amount of useless information he'd taken in over his short lifetime.

Telling the story of his life, following the accident, is like trying to understand a man with Korsakoff syndrome. Every few moments, details merge or new stories branch off in distorted memory.

I, The Narrator, am incapable of telling the story of Ted's life without telling you completely unrelated information. Ted is taken on trips through gravel pits of memory. Everything is an experience. A morning buttering of toast cannot be recalled without his hearing news about slipper thieves and triple homicides.

Ted had become a time traveler, whose vessel was a brain cavity without enough oxygen, unsure of what truly was part of his past or dream.

# 2

## FROM BIRTH

Ted's mother was told that his 'travel' episodes were likely caused by a concussion.

It sounded like the nurse was describing the *Travel Channel*.

Ellen Bundy, mother of Teddy Bundy, was told that micro-sleeping and small seizures often work just as Ted described—blanking out and dreaming.

"But I'm not dreaming. These things happened," Ted said.

Ellen looked down at her feet and said, "People with PTSD can re-experience past events with vivid recollection."

"These events weren't traumatic," Ted said, "I don't think."

"The accident *was* traumatic." Ellen said, again at her shoelaces.

Mike stepped in. "My *dick's* traumatic. Let's shut this shit down."

• • • • • • • • •

Mike was beginning to worry that this seemed like an eerie similarity to what his sister Amanda went through. She had been depressed and believed voices were sometimes saying fairly benign things, such as repeating her name or asking simple questions.

Her psychiatrist's notepad during one session logged one of her recollections. A voice had said the following:

Amanda

A m a n d a

A m a n d a

What are you doing?

Who are you?

Who are you?

Where are you?

What are you doing here?

Who are you? Who are you?

The psychiatrist was alarmed to find that his notes took on the shape of a flaccid phallus. This concerned him about Amanda's well-being.

*Flaccid phallus:* When said rapidly multiple times, the statement is disorienting and difficult to say. If the beautiful voice of The Narrator is to bless an audiobook or public reading, there will be an attempt to say it five times in succession. The first attempt will be the last attempt, unedited.

Amanda was immediately hospitalized and misdiagnosed with schizophrenia. After being heavily medicated, she was apathetic toward living or dying. Mike firmly believed that she chose suicide because she was given a damning diagnosis coupled with the following statement:

> *Think of schizophrenia like diabetes. A diabetic needs insulin, daily, in order to survive and function. Schizophrenia is a disease of the brain. There is no cure. This is your life now.*

Mike, Amanda, and Amanda's psychiatrist were completely unaware that the psychiatric practice of immediately diagnosing auditory hallucinations as schizophrenic was a recent phenomenon. Schizophrenia can be coupled with auditory hallucinations, but they are not exclusive to schizophrenia.

Mark Vonnegut, son of the author Kurt Vonnegut, Jr., wrote a memoir titled *The Eden Express*. He chronicles once having burst into the room of a housemate during a psychotic break. They were good friends. After Mark entered and viciously jerked off the dog sitting next to the bed, his friend was pretty upset.

Friendship has some limits.

Amanda never jerked off a dog, or even a human male for that matter.

She was a lesbian, and though there were no living dongs in her everyday life, there were many a vagina. There had also been many artificial dongs. Some of which took batteries.

· · · ● · ● · ● · · ·

An unpublished poem, by a teenage girl, was once written in lustful "confusion":

>See the beautiful fashion she displays
>With the sunbeams making her radiate love
>And whispers floating sweet upon air
>Through the breeze that carries her soul in waves
>My body's feeling vibrations
>I'm catching all her side glances
>Dreaming now, her breath against my neck
>Pleading words, I hope she hears my ask
>With her eyes piercing through
>Takes me in a field, blooming roses

**Raining Inside**
*A poem by Laura Hitchens*
*Age 16*

This is how Amanda felt with her first love.

The psychiatrist had taken note that Amanda's "confused" sexuality clearly derived from her schizophrenia. Though homosexuality hadn't been included in *The Diagnostic and Statistical Manual of Mental Disorders* since the first version of its delightful criteria, some psychiatrists still believed it to be true.

This is especially the case if they feared the all-seeing eye of a male God above. Amanda's psychiatrist prayed every night, in fear, as he had vivid night terrors of demons that struggled to use can openers. They would blame him for their inability to understand how the human mechanism worked, often cutting themselves in the process.

• • • ● • ● • • •

Back in Ted's hospital room, Mike glared.

Ted laughed. Then Ted began traveling.

"It's happening again," Ted said. "It's happening right now."

Mike excitedly dragged a chair to the bedside. Staring at Ted, he said, "Holy hot shit, drop it on me."

"The year is 1989. I've just been born." Ted said, with some drool sliding down his chin, "My dad is yelling at the nurse."

His dad, Luke, was yelling because Ellen Bundy broke Luke's index finger. She would not let Luke leave her fierce death grip while she gave birth. She was too exhausted to care.

It was April 14, 1989, but it was April 15 in China. A protester had died there of a heart attack. Students were beginning to populate Tiananmen Square.

The nurse handed Teddy to his mother, and Teddy shifted his arms around—grasping at air.

"Whoa, I'm a baby!" Ted said to Mike in 2016.

Ellen looked at baby Teddy in 1989 and recognized him as her son. She smiled. She then recognized him as Luke's son. Her smile left.

Teddy could hear his dad cursing in the hallway outside the room.

Two months prior, a man named Mr. Purdy fired over 100 rounds from an assault rifle. He was aiming down a barrel overlooking an elementary school playground. His hatred for the Asians he believed were secretly invading the country, and taking jobs from white Americans, had taken hold of him. He shot himself with a pistol after shooting over thirty children.

Purdy was quoted once as saying, "I'm dumber than a sixth-grader."

He may have had a chance to be a winner on a popular TV game show that started airing over a decade later, called *Are You Smarter than a 5th Grader?*

He was found with his Chinese-manufactured Type 56 assault rifle, wearing an undamaged flak jacket.

Mr. Purdy is now associated with the Cleveland Elementary School shooting in Stockton, California. This is not to be confused with the Cleveland Elementary School shooting a decade before that, in 1979. That was in another state, and a sixteen-year-old was firing her gun.

Many other notable events happened in 1989.

The Soviets finished withdrawing from Afghanistan, after nine years of occupation.

A dictator in Paraguay was overthrown after thirty-five years in power.

The Berlin Wall fell.

# NOSTALGIA

A British 737 airliner crashed to the earth, killing forty-seven people.

The Australian Prime Minister cried on TV. He admitted to cheating on his wife.

In Tiananmen Square, over 200 protesters were shot dead in the streets.

None of these events had an effect on Teddy's life. Not in 1989, at least. Instead, a man who killed over thirty people within a four-year span had a direct impact. His name was Ted Bundy, and he was just executed in January of that year. A media-inflated serial killer; a sociopath. The bodies of others he killed would remain as cold cases for the years to come.

Teddy is named after that man.

The inventor of the electric chair, used in 1989 to take the life of the serial killer Ted Bundy, was a dentist.

The inventor of the electric toothbrush, as far as history is aware, was not an executioner.

Later in life, Teddy would wonder why he wasn't named after Salvador Dali, who also died that same year. Ted had justification for that sort of question: He had dreams of dogs on the brink of starvation, and clocks melting away into cold soup bowls. He was forced to eat watered-down time with a spork.

"The name is tarnished, but you will bring some kind of good into this life, Teddy," Ellen Bundy said to Ted's squirming little body. Ted's dad walked in and called her a bitch.

The 2016 version Teddy Bundy felt it was earned.

*Serves her right!* Teddy thought. *Who names their kid after a serial killer?*

Luke Bundy then stammered, recovering himself briefly to say that he loved her.

She didn't break away from looking at Teddy, saying, "Don't fuck up, Teddy. Don't you dare."

Ted's dad said, "Teddy? Really?" and asked whether Teddy was a "goddamn teddy bear" before walking over to the window. Luke Bundy kept glancing at the splint on his hand. He was normally a nice man, despite his behavior on the day of Teddy's birth. Luke was a Military Policeman, and he was lucky he was able to witness the birth of his son. Lucky, even if he was kicking and screaming as Teddy entered the world more silent than the surrounding adults.

· · · ● · ● · · ·

Teddy felt himself being pulled out of 1989.

"I'm moving forward," Ted said to Mike. "It's now nineteen ninety-six."

Teddy's in the second grade and the teacher hasn't shown up yet. The children are all waiting at their desks, talking and wondering. Mrs. Larson was his favorite teacher at Point's View Lutheran School.

She was T-boned by a pickup truck, driven by a man trying to beat the light, while on the way to teach her class. She was pronounced dead at the scene. It was Teddy's first confrontation with mortality.

He hadn't even had a gerbil die.

He wore a little angel pin on his favorite jacket at the funeral, inside the church that was connected to the school. Teddy kept the pin and would often imagine that a part of her was contained within it.

It meant she was always with him. Like Jesus. That's what his parents were saying.

A month had passed, Teddy had lost the pin, and he was emotionally shattered.

There was a total of four different teachers that year because of death, sickness, employment termination, and a principal running out of options.

The kids found the principal far too old.

Teddy helped his friend Robbie in the front office of the school. Robbie was getting an extra lunch voucher for his invisible brother Bobby.

The smallest and lightest cellular telephone was released as a wearable mobile that year. It was made by Motorola.

The following year, a Hamas operative would be assassinated by explosives: a rigged cell phone. Cell phones would become rumored as cancer-causing agents by some research entities.

• • • ● • ● • • •

Teddy found himself traveling again. Plucked out of time. Placed somewhere else.

It was 1998. He was eight years old.

A friend of his, Kiefer, had just run straight into a metal pole at recess. They were in the third grade. Kiefer and Teddy were laughing. They couldn't stop their hysterics until they noticed Kiefer's jacket and face were dripping with blood.

Later that day, Teddy's dad was called about a contest to win *Funny Bones*. These things were odd-shape blocks that would glow in the dark, at least the ones in the contest did. Teddy won the sweepstakes at the local Target. Luke Bundy took a detour to pick them up and surprised Teddy after school.

These winnings joined other toys at home, such as his impressive collection of Lego sets and Hot Wheels.

When playing with Legos, Teddy would lose track of time. He would become immersed in his imagination. He often wouldn't hear his parents talking to him.

• • • ● • ● • • •

It was 2010. He was twenty years old.

He was at a park with his girlfriend. He tells her, "My parents deprived me of those life-long friends—you know, brothers or sisters—when they decided their mistake in having me was one mistake too many."

• • • ● • ● • • •

It was 1999. Teddy was ten years old.

Ted doesn't have siblings. The vastness of his made-up stories was all he needed. They evolved into little comics, where one main character was Paperbag Head Man. There was even a theme song where Teddy just repeated, "Paperbag Head Man!" in different tones.

A spinning record.

Nobody knew Paperbag Head Man's true identity because, after a horrific grocery store explosion, the superhero found that he had amazing powers and a disfigured face.

One could guess what his mask was.

A paper bag.

Teddy always had to sing it before reading the comics he made. Teddy's parents were far too aware of this. Eating dinner would often be sound-tracked by this theme song.

Teddy, in 2016, from a hospital bed, said, "Wow. This has been my life."

• • • ● • ● • • •

Ted, becoming conscious of his surroundings, looked around the room. "I'm back in 2016. I'm in my frail, 27-year-old body."

Two nurses had walked in about halfway through his story and were now struggling to get him out of bed.

Ted sent a striking glare at Mike. "A nurse is picking me up to roll me to the bathroom!"

He shifted his piercing eyes to the nurse, continuing, "I tell her that my mom was just wiping my ass a moment ago in nineteen eighty-nine! I also have learned what incontinence means, and that *shitting the bed* isn't just a figure of speech!"

Mike left the room.

He spoke to Teddy's doctor. She tells Mike about bringing in a psychiatrist. Initially, she was thinking of prescribing psychiatric medications early on, especially when Ted first started narrating his past loudly to the nurses.

"Now wait, how many other trips has he had?" Mike asked.

"At least three." The doctor said, visibly counting his fingers, "Maybe more. Remarkably, he is physically okay. He's been banged up, but no fractures. We'll be checking him out again regarding a concussion, but everything looks to check out. He should be able to go home. We have some recommendations for his current state."

# 3

## BACK TO THE WORLD

Teddy was prescribed some medication. The first day he took them, with a bowl of granola and cashew milk, he vomited two hours later. He was told he needed to eat more food to offset the physical effects.

By the third day of vomiting, he could keep it down.

The medications did not eliminate his travels, however, and they only became more dreamlike.

Day two purging of the stomach was met with a fever and a vision in which Teddy watched his grandmother sitting in her rocking chair. She tilted her head back, her mouth gaped open, and black liquid bubbled out across her dress. Tentacles whipped out of her mouth, pulling themselves past her teeth. Her dentures tumbled out across the ever-growing body of a squid emerging from the distant dimension of her stomach.

The man from before—who wanted Ted to be his eyes—was sitting on a couch. He was glancing all around.

"A nightmare of lovely, lovely color," he said.

Teddy's vision went blank as he stopped heaving in the bathroom toilet.

He thought his vision was a little weird.

His mother kept visiting. He had not seen his father at all. This was a normal occurrence. Teddy and his mother imagined Luke Bundy was on another spiritual journey of a bender.

They were right.

Several states away, the old man was sitting in a bar in Colorado. Boulder Beer produced a delicious Shake Chocolate Porter and Luke had arrived at the bar, on pilgrimage, with a trunk full of sticky growlers.

"Livin' the dream," he said to the bartender. "I'm livin' the dream."

Back in Minnesota, Ellen Bundy would come home from work and cry alone in her bedroom. She started sneaking medication from her son in order to try them out herself. With no husband around, and with a message that her son's condition wasn't from brain damage but from "an underlying mental illness," she was falling apart.

This behavior wasn't new. Ellen Bundy's life, in her eyes, was a car crash of disappointment. Her existence was a self-loathing, slow-motion implosion stretching across the past decade.

Teddy, for the most part, was still a functional human being. He wasn't working yet, on medical leave from stocking shelves. The holy help-desk job offer was given to someone else, due to a strict schedule, and Mike had been terminated for taking too many days off to help Ted.

Mike was hitting up new bars to continue his hobby of reviewing restaurants and clubs based on their bathrooms. He was posting something new every week on *Toilet Cafe*.

### BoJak's Tavern: 2 / 5 stars

*It had the sinks where you must push down on the sink head, like you are starting a timer where there is never enough time, and race hands through ice-cold water.*

*After pushing the damn thing down a total of four times, I had enough water on my hands to fail at drying them with the wall dryers. These, at this fine establishment, worked as effectively as an orphan child trying to cough hot air on my hands for some spare change.*

— Reviewed by *MikeMan*

# NOSTALGIA

The CDC recommends twenty seconds to wash one's hands. Mike knows this. Mike took about three seconds of rinsing his slightly soap-stickied hands, a valiant attempt at drying with the air dryer, and then opted to wipe his hands on his pants.

• • • ● • ● • • •

"Thank God," Mike, slightly hungover the next day, said to Ted. "You got all messed up before you quit."

They were in Ted's room at the hospital. Ted grumbled.

"Hey," Mike continued, "do you need a house sitter?"

"Well, I do have a cat back at my apartment that is either dead or will kill you upon entering." Ted said. Mike nodded. Ted went on, "They are also going to be discharging me soon."

"They already have, haven't they?" Mike said.

"My mom is going to discharge me." Ted said.

Mike scoffed, "I can take care of your dumb ass, as long as they give me directions."

Rugged individualism was very much part of the Bundy family philosophy. This meant that any emotional peril, even peril that haunted them into a state of paralysis, was to be fought alone. Under the guise of making each family member stronger, this actually made each of them an island of problems. The family motto could be a combination of "Don't tell anyone" and "None of your business":

> "Don't tell anyone none of your business."
> 
> The Bundy Family

The word "none" can be interpreted as "any" or "some," at times, in the English language.

Here is a snippet extracted, again, from the lovely poet Laura Hitchens:

> My flytrap don't want none,
> unless you got bonbons up front
> and balloons in the trunk.

**Where Tit At?**
*A poem by Laura Hitchens*
*Age 20*

In this poem, "Don't want none" is actually perceived as "Does not want any." Otherwise, it would be a double negative implying that Laura may prefer women with flat tires on the back end.

I speculate that English is very difficult for humans, especially as a second language.

· · · ● · ● · ● · · ·

Soon after Ted's home discharge, he and Mike began a symbiotic relationship. Ted's mother, upon finding out that he was actually okay in the end, had disappeared entirely. His parents had moved several times and changed their numbers whenever they purchased new phones. They had an uncanny ability to provide short-term support and disappear whenever long-term support was required.

A nurse, talking to Ted and Mike on a clinical visit, asked about his parents. "No," Ted said, "Mike will keep helping me out."

"Oh. Are you sure?" she asked.

"Yes," Mike said, "You realize I'm right here, right?"

The nurse didn't respond.

"And why," Mike continued, "do you call it a discharge when we go home from the hospital? Aren't I supposed to come in if I notice any discharge coming out of my—"

"Mike, stop it," Ted said.

Megan let out a loud sigh from the hallway.

Ted knew that Mike and Megan met on an online dating site but was uncertain which one. At that time, there was a boom in sites and applications, as loneliness was prime real estate in a world where people preferred online communication to face to face.

For a better understanding of the available platforms, here is a helpful list:

DickNation<br>
SugarBabbies<br>
Cock/Tail<br>
PocketPoly<br>
WipMePlz<br>
Clitter<br>
JesusFirst<br>
SideThing<br>
GrindHer

At first glance, an unaware individual may guess that these were all porn websites. They assuredly were not. People met human people on them, sometimes cam girls, and sometimes even friendly bots. The really lucky ones, a small percentage of members, met identity theft and blackmail.

Cock/Tail had a dedicated subreddit called Cock/Tales, which had a logo of a rooster reading a book. It was a place for amateur erotic fiction and memoirs. For the past two years, the most popular tales had been edited and published in curated annual collections.

Ted thought maybe they met on Cock/Tail. He never inquired.

Megan sighed again, then asked, "Are we going to leave now?"

"Yeah," Mike said. "We'll be bringing Ted with us."

"Oh." Megan responded, then sighed with her eyes closed.

"What do you mean by 'Oh'?" Mike pushed.

"Nothing. I just meant 'Oh'." Megan said, keeping her eyes closed.

Megan was fairly introverted and valued her alone space. Her communication was normally passive, which had made Mike overly sensitive to her responses. She had a steady supply of THC and CBD in her system on a daily basis, due to a chronic illness she never disclosed, and this had blunted her communication style even further.

The Narrator, a benevolent revealer, knows that Mike had not met Megan on any of the available dating applications out there. Mike used a different type of application that had also brought many people together: a video game. *War Gods*, a graphics-intensive, subscription-based online game. A few months into the game, Mike came across a character set up with amazing gear. What he didn't realize was that this character was not being played by an actual person.

Megan had developed a bot to respond to basic types of questions with responses that were similar to her personality type. She had recorded all conversations she had ever had with people online via the game, and she taught a bot to replicate her personality. It took three weeks of conversation with the bot before Mike was noticed by

Megan. She had seen, statistically, that one of her bots was having an excessive amount of communication back and forth with the same player.

She started to take over for the bot, when it came to text chat, by redirecting communications to a custom application on her active laptop. While her bot played the game for her, increasing player stats and in-game gold, she was able to type in a little window while she scrolled over webcam access portals on BetaSea. Several hacking groups had banded together and spread malware purely for the purpose of taking over other people's webcams, then sold "view-only" access on the dark net. This was a win-win situation for hackers and customers: Hackers kept access open to these webcams, and customers paid to see people of all ages sitting in front of a screen.

The seller page would include a screenshot of the laptop owner, with gender and age. Age was gained via the malware, which monitored websites that prompted the user for information. Using a specialized lookup service for external IP addresses, along with the information he had posted to the game console logs, Megan discovered that Mike's laptop was one of the systems that had been compromised. She watched Mike periodically via his webcam before proposing that they meet, as they happened to win the bizarre lottery of both being in Chisago County, Minnesota.

Megan knew everything about Mike and had even seen Ted several times. She had four months' worth of silent stalking and bot-generated conversations. Mike had provided so much personal information to the bot that she never had to initiate conversation to learn more about him, especially as his Facebook profile was publicly viewable.

Social media was a gift from the gods to stalkers around the world, a collaborative effort with Narcissus himself.

They met, and less than a month later, Mike had moved in with Megan. He was behind on rent in a shared house and was happy to get the hell out. Megan had lived alone for the past six years, and she felt that maybe he would help her out of the crushing loneliness from which black-market consumerism wasn't able to save her.

She was wrong.

When Mike suggested that he live with Ted to take care of things, she realized this was an amazing opportunity to save the relationship, along with her personal space.

It wasn't an easy transition for Ted. He checked out as a perfectly healthy man, and was recommended to see a neurologist, who then scheduled him for a sleep study. This was when Ted realized that, with his sub-par health insurance, he had already racked up considerable debt. He thanked the neurologist for his time and never went to the sleep study.

The doctor told him that he should at least see a well-known psychiatrist in the area, who would likely take Ted on pro bono, in the event that his issue was more psychological than neurological.

"You should really see this guy, Ted," the doctor said. "His name is Dr. Simon Kant."

Ted agreed to meet him.

If Mike had heard this exchange, a blackout of rage may have consumed him into changing Ted's mind by threat of death. This did not happen.

Ted's apartment was a 610-square-foot one-bedroom apartment, with a small office room that became Mike's sleeping quarters. Thankfully for Ted, his work continued to send him paychecks during his medical leave. Even though he had a daunting mountain of medical debt, he wasn't going to be evicted.

Unknown to him, he was in a better financial state than most college dropouts and graduates. What Ted didn't realize was that his $26,315.48 worth of medical expenses not covered by insurance was still less than the average student loan debt in the United States, which was over $30,000.

Some get debt from college. Ted went to the hospital for his.

A man named Ryan Williams lived in the apartment above Ted. He had incurred $80,000 worth of debt by attending university in River Falls, Wisconsin. Six high-school students periodically visited as a group, of which Ryan only personally knew one: his girlfriend, Elizabeth.

*"I think, therefore I am [a thingy]."*
René Descartes

René is a beautiful name. I imagine he was a beautiful thingy.

A teenager sitting next to Ryan handed over a needle. "Here, take this thingy and stick it in your arm."

It would help relieve that stress and anxiety of being a thingy.

So Ryan went ahead and did as he was told.

Student loans, credit cards, family, war, child soldiers, genocide, the sex trade, diarrhea, even the clap, all ceased to be. He felt like he was no longer a thingy, too. He was just a blob in the pleasure pit of meaningless existence. Pure feel. Zero mind. Heroin was the great release.

"It's like being cradled to sleep in the arms of God," he was told. Feeling was believing.

In the Bible, God is capable of deploying the angel of death. In serious cases, he just does it himself—cradling his creations to the deep sleep of forever after. By the end of 2016, nearly five hundred deaths were to be documented in Minnesota as being opioid related. One hundred fifty of those were related to heroin.

# 4

## A Vision and a Psychiatrist

At Ted's place, Mike was applying for jobs online. He had an interview next week in a warehouse for a massive online distributor. Ted's cat, an orange tabby named Carl, kept his distance. Carl would meow at people and always walk just beyond reach. At times, he would suddenly run, and hope that something—anything—would chase him around. Mike and Ted never did.

Carl ran around with imaginary animal friends to make up for this deficit.

Carl is ignored so egregiously that The Narrator has now lost complete interest in his presence and will avoid mentioning him ever again.

"Well, at least there are larger gaps between your flashbacks," Mike said.

"Sure," Ted said, "and here we go again."

Ted stood still in the middle of the living room.

"Right now?" Mike asked.

"Yeah. It's weird, though." Ted went on, "There's a guy sitting on a porch. He's at a house that's surrounded by looming trees. There's a baby-blue pickup truck sitting in the front yard."

Mike walked Ted over to a chair and sat him down as he continued talking. Ted's eyes didn't roll back into his head, or close. They just stared off into the distance.

"Hold on, let me write this down." Mike started scribbling almost illegible handwriting on a notepad.

"I don't think I'm in my past, or having one of those weird dreams." Ted said, narrowing his eyes, "I'm just watching a guy reading a book. Someone just parked in the driveway and is walking toward him."

Ted watched, from a fixed point of view, over the shoulder of the man reading. He could see another man approaching, wearing a black T-shirt and camo pants. His hair was past his shoulders, a bit unkempt. The reader gave a slight acknowledgment to the person walking toward him but continued reading.

"I think they must know each other, like this is just a normal visit maybe," Ted said.

Ted couldn't quite see it, but the person walking up to the house was carrying something. He disappeared from view. The sound of heavy boots started on the porch, just outside his field of vision.

The reader said, "You really coming back? I already told you, I'm—"

The approaching man stepped into view again. He was holding a crossbow, and he was shaking, his eyes bloodshot.

"Holy fuck, Dick, what— what is this?" The reader stood up from his chair.

He dropped after an arrow went through his leg. He was yelling in complete confusion.

"That's what," Dick said, lowering the crossbow. He walked back toward his truck. The sky was clear, and the world was still.

Ted relayed everything to Mike, gaining ahold of himself and his apartment surroundings again.

"Wow," Mike said, "Was his name Dick, like Dick Cheney, or was he being called a dick?"

"I think his name was Dick." Ted said.

"Huh. Not sure how to interpret that one." Mike said, before snapping his fingers, "We should get a dream dictionary. I used to have one by this guy Dr. Phissure, and—"

"No." Ted grumbled.

"Why not?" Mike asked.

"People don't just look at dream dictionaries to interpret things like, I don't know," Ted said, waving his hands around, "hallucinations and flashbacks."

"Why not?" Mike asked again.

Ted waved his hands again, more erratically, saying, "They just don't!"

"You should tell your psychiatrist about it, then." Mike said, with a smirk, "Maybe he'll mash some tranquilizers down your throat. I don't know why you're thinking that's going to help anything."

"This isn't something I can simply change my diet for, Mike. I'm looking for whatever can help, honestly. I just want to live a normal life. What if this doesn't stop? What if it's life-long?"

Mike sighed. He had nothing to say.

Mike brewed a pot of coffee every day due to a feeling that Ted's condition was worsening. He thought it could help. Ted tried to keep himself present by dosing himself with as much caffeine as possible. This didn't work. He told Mike about everything he was seeing. When he met with Dr. Simon Kant, he repeated his experiences.

• • • • ● • ● • • •

His latest travel experience brought him to a public library in 2010. He was twenty-one years old, staring at the printer that he paid twenty cents to use.

Page one came out just fine. Two strange pages printed out next, followed by his page two. He was horrified. The mystery pages seemed to reflect the insanity of the past week.

They were covered with speckled, unmoving static dots, and lines of all lengths, creating scattered labyrinths across the page. A form of abstract art was now in his possession, as though created by supernatural elements haunting his environment.

Did he possess the papers, or did the papers possess him?

He was afraid he'd become lost in an introspective maze if he tried to look for some kind of meaning in the images.

Leading up to the printer incident, Mike and Ted had been experiencing what they would later dub hell week. Ted had mentioned an idea for a graphic novel of some sort, where messages were communicated to people via speckled imagery. Anything from the white-snow static of analogue TVs, to scattered dots sometimes stamped onto physical mail.

They were talking over VoIP about the idea, but then Mike couldn't hear Ted anymore. The call had become an extremely loud electronic garble. Using a separate application, Ted tested his microphone. Indeed, it was far too sensitive and loud. If he spoke, his speakers would blare out nonsense. If he sat silently, he could hear something in the background. People were talking. Ted lived alone.

Speaking to Mike over the phone, Ted relayed the oddity. It jolted the two of them.

"This is like *The Twilight Zone*, Mike," Ted said.

"Right. Well, it's late." Mike said, yawning, "Let's just talk tomorrow."

Mike flipped on his TV after hanging up. The first words that came from the system were, "Welcome to...The Twilight Zone." A twenty-four-hour marathon had just started.

The two sent messages to each other daily.

Both would find themselves abruptly waking up, with their quality of sleep continuously degrading.

A black dog had appeared in Mike's backyard, staring silently into his window during a thunderstorm. If this did not literally happen, the reader may find themselves believing The Narrator was merely speaking in metaphor. The Narrator isn't. The goddamn dog scared the shit out of Mike's scrambled brain.

Ted had found a strange news article about how an organization had just spent billions of dollars on broadcast television waves. The FCC had auctioned them off via the "Spectrum Act" passed in 2012. *They are buying up the air, where the messages are getting caught and swallowed up,* he thought. The word "swallowed" came to mind because he was eating soggy fruit loops, and he imagined his ear holes eating invisible fruit loops of the air. Fruit loops corrupted and soggy from the billions of dollars interfering, seeking his interest.

Mike found himself running to a bus stop while being chased by the same black dog.

Ted, while driving home after a Member$Mart night shift, had nearly hit a man walking in the middle of the road with no shirt on.

The man was albino, and startled Ted into nearly crashing his car as he swerved to avoid him.

The lack of sleep seemed to make Ted's brain matter porous, riddled with holes eager to soak up the world surround. Unfocused, uncontrolled powers that seemed to foreshadow what was to become of him after his accident.

Foreshadowing is a literary device meant to hint to the reader about something, and The Narrator feels the need to spell this out.

### F.O.R.E.S.H.A.D.O.W.I.N.G.

*An acrostic is a poem that spells a word when combining the first letters of every line.*

**F**unky
**O**vertures
**R**eveal
**E**xciting
**S**ecrets
**H**idden
**A**cross
**D**esperate
**O**h
**W**hat the fuck
**I** don't know how to finish this, so, uh
**N**arcoleptic
**G**uy

Dr. Simon Kant, leaning back excessively in his office chair, asked Ted, "So, you see past events every time?"

"Most of the time," Ted said.

Leaning back impossibly further, Kant let out a slight, "Hm?"

"Sometimes it's just a really weird dream. Other times," Ted said, reaching for words by drawing circles in the air, "I'm not in it. It's like I'm in the future or something, but I've already died so now I'm seeing things that happen later on."

Kant began slowly leaning forward in his chair, saying, "How far in the future do you believe this is?"

"I don't think it's far. The same news anchors are on TV, cars look the same, people talk and dress the same." Ted said.

He had seen glimpses of a news special that referenced a group of women and a suicide. Whether the suicide was deliberate or not? Unclear. Other than that, he had seen a slow-motion truck commercial in which a man in rugged clothing towed construction equipment to a soundtrack of rock music.

"Do you believe you will die soon?" Dr. Simon Kant asked, now in an upright position.

"I don't know." Ted said, then whispered under his breath, "I don't want to think about it."

"Well, we all die," said Dr. Simon Kant. "It's a fact of life." Kant was now leaning forward toward Ted.

"Okay." Ted said.

Kant, locked in a stare with Ted, asked, "Can you give me an example of one of your – as you called them – weird dreams?"

Ted told him about a dream in which he was an anteater that dressed, talked, and walked upright like a human. He was walking through a forest, in a business suit, past a little cabin. The cabin window popped open, and a man stuck his head out. This man was a coworker at Member$Mart, named Franklin. In the dream, Franklin stared apathetically at Ted the anteater.

In this dreamworld, this brought on some form of flashback, in which the anteater was attempting to cross a raging river while carrying a woman. The current picked up, the anteater lost his footing, and the woman was swept away.

This woman was cabin-Franklin's wife.

After struggling to get over a flooded area of still water, by jumping across moss-covered platforms that floated around, Ted made it to his destination. Three unrecognizable creatures stood behind looming podiums, asking the anteater if he was ready for what was about to come next.

"Which was?" Dr. Simon Kant prodded. He leaned forward and then remained absolutely still. He was clearly enthralled in the story.

"Which was when I woke up," Ted said.

"That's unfortunate." Kant said, breaking the stare and slouching, "The worst stories end with 'then I woke up' don't they?"

What Ted didn't realize was that Simon believed he could find the secret to resolving issues in his own dreams by attempting to adopt the bizarre outcomes of his patients' dreams. He felt that maybe there was a form of collective unconscious in which truths about the world would be revealed through others' dreams. He had seen a YouTube video about Jung and, without researching what Jung's actual thoughts were on the matter, had made assumptions as to what Jung meant.

"So I understand that you are in a rough spot when it comes to finances," Dr. Simon Kant continued. "You have also said that your physical health checks out. Well, I would like to prescribe you some medications to see if they may assist in suppressing this traveling of yours. It sounds a bit like a bounce between schizophrenia and PTSD, but let's not go nuts here. Medication shouldn't be your only approach, by the way. There is a sliding scale group therapy that I know of, and there is also a phenomenal group of people that meet in Minneapolis. They call themselves biohackers."

Ted squinted.

"Right," Kant said, "it really just means improving your life by way of exercise and diet, from what I've seen. It's a great idea and would be a good start. I'd love to have another chat. Oh! So, before we jump on the prescription medication train, you should take some of these free samples."

The box said aripiprazole.

"Just follow the directions there," Dr. Simon Kant said to Ted, "and we'll see where you're at in a week or two."

By this point Ted couldn't drive anymore, as he was worried he would drop into the '90s before crashing into oncoming traffic in 2016.

• • • ● • ● • • •

Mike was sitting in the lobby, across from two other men chatting.

Unaware what the two were talking about, Mike was listening to music on headphones with his eyes closed. He opened his eyes to see the two laughing, caught in intense conversation, and then one of them handed over a business card to the other. They shook hands, grinning like long-lost friends reconnecting, and looked over to see Ted step out of Dr. Simon Kant's office.

Mike and Ted nodded at one another, and left.

• • • ● • ● • • •

Dr. Simon Kant stepped outside his office, into the waiting room, and was bewildered to see the two men in his lobby. Kant said, with his eyes shot wide, "Oh fuck, did I schedule the two of you together at the same time?"

The two men, along with Dr. Simon Kant, were startled by his use of a curse word in such a professional setting.

"No worries," one of them said, putting the business card he was given into his pocket. "I'll follow up to reschedule, Simon. Fate brought us together today."

"Rescheduling sounds fine, James," Kant said, "but I don't think you should talk to Johnathan—"

"It's okay, Doc," Johnathan interrupted. "It was meant to happen. I've given him my business card."

James left, shaking his head in astonishment and laughter.

"What was that about? When did you get business cards?" Dr. Simon Kant asked Johnathan.

"Just last week." Johnathan responded, "Here, have one."

**JOHNATHAN** JESUS CHRIST
THE MESSIAH

*Front*

**GOD** SAID SO
    AND I AGREE

*Back*

"James is a remarkable man," Johnathan said to Dr. Simon Kant, who grew pale the more he realized the ramifications of his mistake. "He asked if I heard the voice of God, like he does. I stared into his soul, Doc, and I said this: No, I am the one who speaks it."

## 5

## SLEEP PARALYSIS

"Wow, what happened?" Mike said, looking out Ted's apartment window. An ambulance had screamed up into the parking lot a few minutes ago. A gurney, carrying a sheet-covered body, was being raised into the back.

"The guy who lives above me was found dead and blue in the stairwell," Ted said.

Ryan Williams, sole tenant of apartment 602, had died after sticking another thingy of heroin in his arm. In fear, his high school friends dragged his unconscious body down what they felt was safer than an elevator. Their goal had been to get his body to a car parked outside so that they could plop him on the pavement outside a hospital. Someone had entered the stairwell from a few floors above, and as their footsteps came closer, scared them away.

Unfortunately for Ryan, the stranger exited the stairwell exactly one floor above where his body lay. He wouldn't be found until the following morning, by a building maintenance man, by which time he would be dead.

Dealers were getting ahold of an animal tranquilizer called carfentanil and lacing their products. It was being sold online all over the world from China, where it was still legal to produce and distribute.

It was meant to knock an elephant unconscious for surgery. All it could do for a human, really, was kill them. The strength was said to be one hundred times stronger than fentanyl, or ten thousand times stronger than morphine.

Two drops, the size of grains of salt, could kill a man.

The latest batch injected into Ryan's arm had included a trace of the fatal drug.

It was like being cradled to death in the arms of God.

In the future, in 2017, sting operations in Canada would uncover carfentanil blotter tabs called "drop dead." In 2019, a couple would be arrested with enough carfentanil in their possession that could kill over an estimated one million people.

· · · ● · ● · ● ● · ·

"Placebos?" Ted asked, with spit flying out of his mouth.

"Yes," Dr. Simon Kant said, with complete lack of emotion. "I needed to be sure, since you said you were fine physically."

"I was told to see a neurologist," Ted said, turning red, "I was at the end of the line when it came to how much debt I could take on. I have to go back to work in a week if I want to keep getting a paycheck. I'm hitting the limit of paid medical leave."

"Well, good news." Kant said, with a smile, "In my opinion, it would have been a complete waste. I know exactly what's wrong with you."

Ted stared, still red, in wait.

Kant said, while looking at the wall, "You have been developing schizophrenia."

"Even taking into account my car accident?" Ted asked.

"You were already told you are physically fine. I believe you have a form of mental trauma that your mind continues to erase." Dr. Simon Kant was talking to the ceiling now, as though presenting his brilliance to the heavens. "Your mind wishes it can literally go back in time, before the accident, and before you became so apathetic about life."

Ted was no longer red, but was instead growing pale, and said, "Apathetic?"

"You stock shelves, don't feel any drive toward higher education, don't want to even be promoted to a higher position at Member$Mart," Kant said, counting his list on an open hand facing Ted, "and your relationships are driven by anybody other than yourself."

"Now wait a minute," Ted started.

"Remind me, what was the reason Laura gave?" Kant said, looking back at his desk and shuffling through blank papers, "The reason for leaving you?"

"My condition has nothing to do with Laura." Ted said, the red returning to his face in a creeping wave.

"Fine." Kant said, shuffling some papers off his desk to the floor, "For now, let's let sleeping dogs tell lies."

"You mean *let sleeping dogs lie.*" Ted said.

"That's what I said. Man's best friend is a liar." Kant said, with the kind of smug smile someone carries when they feel they've said something profound, "Anyway, we are just about out of time for today, Ted. You can pick up a proper prescription from reception. Unlike the placebo, there are actual side effects to keep in mind with these."

Dr. Simon Kant picked a piece of paper off the floor. He started reading, rather flatly, a list of potential problems that could arise.

This included a rather long list of potential issues related to muscle control, such as tremors and partial paralysis. He enunciated the final item on the list, *neuroleptic malignant syndrome*, very slowly.

"Yes," Kant continued, "if you notice a complete loss of feeling with certain muscles, drooping of the face, or fevers and the like, you should stop taking it immediately. These can be a symptom of a potentially fatal condition." He gave a brief laugh, but caught himself and stared at his lap in embarrassment.

"Did you just laugh?" Ted said.

"No." Kant said, looking back to the ceiling.

"Did you say I could die?" Ted said, his face receding back to pale.

"Now, Ted, the benefits outweigh the risks. Take the medication." Kant said, keeping his eyes on a spot in the ceiling tiles. The spot looked like a demon his recognized in his dreams. "It is meant to be temporary, to help bring things under control. We're out of time. Please schedule a follow-up at reception."

Ted walked out of the office with a prescription paper in his hand, strolled into the lobby, and then to reception. He had tunnel vision, and his body was on autopilot. He had an exchange of words with reception, and he was given some papers along with a complimentary DVD. It was a film about other patients with similar conditions. In it, Ted was assured, he would learn of a man named Amir. Amir had catatonic schizophrenia but was awakened with medication. He believed he was a tiger, living and hunting in a forest, before taking the antipsychotic prescribed to Ted. Amir was now able to function as a "contributing member of society" by bagging groceries and living with his brother.

The Narrator knows all things. Ted did not. What the film did not reveal was that Amir missed the forest life at times because of the simplicity of it. He wasn't a human thingy when living in the universe that was compiled by his brain. It was a grand form of escapism that didn't cost a dime. Student loans, credit cards, family, war, child soldiers, genocide, the sex trade, diarrhea, and even the clap all ceased to be in that place.

Ted's neighbor, Ryan, would have gotten along well with Amir.

Elephant tranquilizers made this an impossibility, but The Narrator wonders about the effects that carfentanil has on tigers both real and imagined.

The Narrator also wonders whether his disembodied self could have been created with a moral compass better aligned with that of humanity. A quick search of current events on the internet, at any point in time, helps suppress that thought by showing humanity to be capable of being terribly cruel to itself.

The Narrator, having just used *his* as a pronoun for himself, has come to understand that perhaps nonbinary is a better qualifier for his gender. He does not care. He/Him. He/Haw. He/llo. May the human gods have mercy on the editors of this manuscript.

Speaking of oneself in the third person is quite exciting.

· · · • · • · · ·

When Ted made it home, driven once more by Mike as his chauffeur, he stared at the wall. Sleep came slowly that night. He took 20 mg of aripiprazole in the morning. Ted wasn't fully aware that this was a rather high dose, one that he was meant to raise to 30 mg over the next three days. Dr. Simon Kant felt that Ted needed to reach the maximum dose rather quickly, in accordance with the suggestion of a demon that plagued the dreams of the psychiatrist.

Ted, eating a bowl of cereal while Mike searched for jobs on his laptop, found himself traveling again. This time, the pull felt like he was being dragged out of his skull. He noticed a loss of feeling in his legs, and his neck was having difficulty holding his head up.

•  •  •  ●  ●  •  ●  •  •  ·

He was twenty-two years old, watching television in 2011. He was in his apartment, being shown the greatest hits of absurdity that circulated the Obama administration.

Ted's traveling experiences made him realize how often he did nothing productive. Many of his memories involved hours of floating around the internet, watching television, or playing video games. Sometimes, he just found himself lying in bed and staring at the wall as anxieties bombarded his sleepless mind.

This time, it was another mind-numbing experience of sitting uncomfortably on a sofa with his ex, Laura.

"You gotta be kidding me," she said, shaking her head.

The documentary was reviewing all the Republican statements regarding "death panels" that were going to be put into place if the Patient Protection and Affordable Care Act (ACA! Another acronym!) was passed—often referred to as Obamacare.

Sarah Palin had said that Americans "will have to stand in front of Obama's 'death panel' so his bureaucrats can decide, based on a subjective judgment of their 'level of productivity in society,' whether they are worthy of health care."

"How could people believe any of that?" Laura said.

"Because an opponent of his is saying it, I suppose," Ted said.

Laura tilted her head, and said, "This doesn't piss you off?"

"It does. I guess. Not really," Ted said. "Hasn't it always been ridiculous?"

Laura scoffed, and continued staring at the screen.

"Ted," a woman standing in the doorway said, "we need to talk."

Ted didn't recognize the woman. He then found himself standing beside the sofa, looking at his past self sitting next to Laura. The pair on the sofa didn't react to the stranger's presence, and Ted felt weirdly detached from the situation.

"What's happening?" Ted said, watching his silent self staring at the television.

"Ted, we need to talk," the woman said again.

Laura tilted her head, and said, "This doesn't piss you off?"

"It does. I guess. Not really," Ted said. "Hasn't it always been ridiculous?"

Laura scoffed, and continued staring at the screen.

"Ted," a woman standing in the doorway said, "we need to talk."

Ted pulled his attention back. "I feel like I'm torn between my own experiences and trying to listen to you. Mike! Hey, Mike! This one is a crazy one."

"Who's Mike?" Sara asked.

There was no response. Ted wondered if Mike may have left the room. Now music came from the living room. Ted stepped over to take a look inside and saw a birth certificate spinning around on the television screen. Laura and his past self laughed together, holding each other closer.

Ted felt needles in his chest. He had become utterly codependent on Laura at one point, and she had felt suffocated by him when she ended their relationship.

Sara spoke as though in a hurry. "Ted, stop getting distracted. You need to listen to me. I'm not the only one."

"Seriously?" Ted said, "What is he doing with you?"

"This," she said. She stared at Ted.

"Okay? What?" Ted said.

Sara opened her eyes wide. She lifted her hands to her face. Black circles appeared around her eyes, and bloody tears dripped down her face.

"This!" she screamed. Her hands closed into trembling fists. "This! This! This!"

Screaming came from the living room. Ted ran in. On the television screen he saw Mr. Satin stepping away from a woman lying unconscious on a table. Laura and his past self were falling off the couch in convulsions, bleeding from their eyes.

• • • ● • ● • • •

Ted woke up with his face pressed against the table. Mike was wiping up milk and cereal that had spilled everywhere.

When Ted tried to move, his body didn't respond. He wondered whether this is what people felt when they found themselves newly paralyzed: identifying with ghosts that flail phantom arms in the prison of a shell of flesh.

A woman pulled out the chair next to him and sat in it. It was Sara. Droplets of blood were still rolling down her face.

"This! This! This!" she kept shouting at him.

Ted grunted. He gained enough control over his body to raise his head up.

Sara was no longer there.

# 6

## Premonitions

"Glad you're back," Mike said. "You did a face-plant into your bowl of cereal and started making gurgling noises. If I wasn't here, you could have drowned in your fucking Lucky Charms. Why do you eat that shit? I'm Irish, you know. It's insulting."

Ted wiped drool and milk off his face, then said, "If this is due to the medication, I'm not taking it anymore. What if I was opening the stove or something? I'd be dead."

"Thankfully you don't know how to cook," Mike shrugged, "so that would never happen."

As Ted's concerns grew, he found he was losing the ability to speak. He had too many thoughts at once, tangling themselves up in knots that would confuse an Eagle Scout. By the time he opened his mouth, he could barely recall his dream.

Mike seemed unsympathetic to a degree that Ted wasn't expecting.

"I just passed out, Mike. Jesus," Ted said, "shouldn't we be worried about this?"

"We?" Mike asked. "*You* should. If I'm around, I'll help save you from yourself, but you're going to need to get some kind of social worker. You need to take your condition way more seriously than you have been. Medical debt or not, this isn't just a cold. Man, maybe try and get a hold of your mom. It's not like she's doing anything."

So Ted did. He was surprised to find she hadn't changed her number yet.

"Hello?" Ellen Bundy said, "Teddy? Is something wrong?"

He explained everything. His doctor, the neurologist and the recommendation for a sleep study, his psychiatrist, and his collapse into his childish breakfast cereal.

"Wow," she said. "Have you talked to your dad at all?"

"No. How is he?" Ted asked.

"I don't know." Ellen said, sighing, "I haven't seen him for the past three months. He just disappeared."

"What the hell, Mom?" Ted said, shaking his head, "Did you call the police at least? File a missing person's report or something?"

"I haven't seen him but I've talked to him." Ellen said, shakily, "He calls me now and then."

"Really?" Ted said, "What does he say?"

"That life is really good. He says it in a strong, sober, peaceful way. I think he has finally found some peace, Ted." Ellen said.

The Narrator would like to state that this was a bald-faced lie.

The Narrator would also like to ask why there aren't *shaggy-faced* lies, or *shaved-faced* lies, and whether a bald-faced lie would be the worst kind.

Some people want facial hair, others do not.

*Face Blindness* is a known neurological phenomenon where a person cannot recognize a person by their face. The Narrator would like to create a simulated world where *Male Pattern Face Blind-*

*ness* exists, and people struggle to remember the faces of male humans.

As for Ted believing his mom in this conversation, about his father being at sobered peace, he did not believe a word.

Ellen continued. "He told me he was keeping in touch with you, so I'm mad at him for lying about that."

Ted's father was often heavily drunk when he called, sobbing unintelligible statements of remorse and promises of change. He normally claimed he was checking in on their son.

"Good ol' Al," Luke Bundy would say about Ted. "Al always knew how to live a good life. I'm proud of that boy. I tell him every week."

He had never called Ted. Luke wasn't even aware of Ted having been in an accident.

Luke called Ted by his middle name, Al for Alex, because of the tie to *Married... with Children*. He felt that was a more reasonable template for Ted's upbringing, instead of introducing a little serial killer to strangers.

"You like the Vikings, right?" Ellen asked Ted.

"The football team?" Ted asked.

"Yeah." Ellen said.

"No." Ted said.

"Yeah you do!" Ellen blurted out, "Why are you saying no? Well, I sent you a present in the mail."

"Mom, I need some serious help." Ted said, "I passed out today, and I think it was due to my medication. I couldn't even move when I woke up, and I thought a woman was yelling at me. She wasn't even there. I'm not really sure what to do here."

"Get more sleep." Ellen said, triumphantly, "Enjoy the gift, Ted. It should come today! Love you!"

She hung up. Ted tried calling back, but it went to voicemail.

• • • ● • ● • • •

Ellen had blocked Ted's number and was getting into her car to get her number changed at the local, helpful phone distributor.

• • • ● • ● • • •

Ted dropped the phone and felt himself drifting.

"This. Again. Happening now," Ted said.

"Ted, stop what you're doing! You gotta hear this!" Mike said.

"Right, great idea, I'll just stop it," Ted said, collapsing on his couch.

• • • ● • ● • • •

"I'm glad you're here again, Ted," Mr. Satin said.

"You know my name?" Ted said, "Christ, have you really been stalking me?"

Mr. Satin scoffed, then said, "Stalking you? If anything, you have been stalking me. I've had no choice in the matter. You practically destroyed a toilet in one of our shared experiences. You were a little kid that time. Not sure what your dream was about, but there was a funeral, I think."

"This is just a dream." Ted said, wagging his finger.

"If it is, then my existence was made purely by your broken head." Mr. Satin said, smiling, "It seems like sometimes you are seeing me, sometimes you are seeing some part of your past, and sometimes you are just having a trippy-as-fuck dream. Sometimes they blend together. I want you to know that what you are seeing right now is very real."

"Uh, okay." Ted said, looking around.

"It's not a dream or lie. It's super real." Mr. Satin said, throwing his arms up.

Ted laughed, then said, "You are making it seem less likely that—"

"Ted," Mr. Satin interrupted, "I need you to tell me where you are from. Where do you live?"

"Why?" Ted asked.

"You want to save lives, don't you?" Mr. Satin asked back, "Do you just perpetually ask questions? I know for a fact that you've seen me talking about *killing* people. I'm much more to fear than a run-of-the-mill bitcoin hitman."

"No." Ted said, "I don't have any crypto, and I'm not telling you anything."

"So much beautiful color going to waste." Mr. Satin said, with a sigh, "Fine. Let me show you something fantastic."

Mr. Satin began making his way across the crosswalk, into oncoming traffic. A minivan, driven by a man distracted by a lengthy text about how bananas are a symptom of globalism, was driving full-speed. Mr. Satin opened his mouth, his eyes slightly closed, and he lifted his arm as if to ward off the minivan. The hood smashed downward, as though stomped by an unseen beast, and the distracted driver was propelled through the windshield.

Time crawled.

Ted could hear scattered words and thoughts that weren't his, but they were overtaken by the audible thoughts of the pedestrian-turned-human-missile. The driver had somehow entered the same time-space as Ted, and at the most inopportune time.

### THE THOUGHTS OF ZACK CLARKSON

*Oh my God.*
*God.*
*Oh my God.*
*What.*
*What's happening.*
*Holy sweet ugly shit.*

That went on for a while. Ted felt horrible for the man, because Ted felt that the man was slowly experiencing what likely was his death.

### THE THOUGHTS OF ZACK CLARKSON (CONT.)

*Oh fuck.*
*Wait.*
*Shit.*
*I don't have my license.*
*Will they know who I am?*
*The car. They could look at the car and find the owner.*
*Shitty dick.*
*They'll find it's not mine, that it's Cynthia's fucking car.*
*God dammit. Dammit dammit dammit.*

*My phone. There it is. It's flopping through the air on the charger.*

*If I'm unconscious, my phone is locked. Nobody knows the password. Nobody.*

*They won't know it. What if I have to tell a doctor to unlock it? I don't know anybody's number. It's all in the fucking phone.*

*I'd have to tell them the password.*

### j@ckoff12345done

*God.*
*If I die?*
*Motherfucker.*

*I should have wrote my email password in a will, or under my fucking pillow. I should have had that password somewhere for people to read. Wait, the first letter must be capitalized.*

### J@ckoff12345done

*It will be horrible. Reading my will off to my wife, knowing I was driving Cynthia's van, probably knowing I was fucking Cynthia, and then being told the password. How would they explain this when going over my will?*

# NOSTALGIA

"I leave my email to access all of my assets online, with the following password to be given to my beautiful, loving wife."

### J@ckoff12345done

"Yes, that's really what Zach wrote. I am sorry, but that's what it is. I know. Zach was a dick. Clearly. Actually, he wasn't a dick. He was a pile of dick shit. I think instead of a coffin, you can choose the affordable option of just hurling his body into those massive piles of manure that build up at farms. You know, those farms that have atrocious conditions for their cows? Where the runoff caused salmonella outbreaks in spinach? It's green, organic, and an expression of your hatred for him. Especially because you'd be ignoring the state of meat harvesting all the while."

Fuck. What about Dennis? He's still at school. Nobody will pick him up. What.

What the fuck is this!
Oh God!
Yeeeeeeeeeee!

Zach screamed in agony for a full five minutes in Ted Time, before Zach's ejected body met a street sign.

It was a "hello, goodbye" sort of meeting.

• • • ● • ● • ● • •

What Zach didn't know, and wouldn't ever know, is that he had accidentally been saving the naked pictures of himself that he'd been sending to his mistress. This feature had been enabled for the past four months, saving to a default online picture folder, per his phone's helpful operating system.

An entire secret, online album was dedicated to his dick and pictures of sports cars he passed on the bus.

I, The Narrator, know this because I have incredible insight into meaningless information. I can confirm that at least it didn't synchronize with Zach's Facebook page, like when his sister Vivian had accidentally uploaded multiple pictures in bulk. Her feed blew up with likes, shares, and her dad's comments displaying confused disappointment.

Normally a gentle, polite Minnesotan, Vivian's father was beside himself in what he felt was a public statement of his failure as a parent. To defend his honor, and extremely out of character, he even went as far as posting a public comment.

> *I've done everything for you, and look at what you choose to be... a whore.*

Her ex responded to her father's comment with a display of his condolences and his public education.

> *yeayuh i tapped dat @$$. plz post moar. gotta fap*

Ted wanted to wake up. Travel back home.

"You can call me Mr. Satin, Ted," the man with rounded blue sunglasses said, "because that is all I see most of the time. The world is normally just a satin hue to me. You, though, you bring color! I mean, look at this."

Ted had no idea what to say, still trying to comprehend what was happening. Mr. Satin walked over to Zach's body, surrounded by blood and glass.

"Red! Look at the red!" Mr. Satin said, overtaken by an exhilarating mania. "I mean, I've been able to dream in color for a good while now. My brain certainly remembers and is completely capable of showing me it when I'm unconscious. I can even dream in first person at times."

Ted started traveling deeper.

He was breaking open a panel on a large structure he had climbed up, alongside a woman who was explaining to him that he needed to flip all the switches off in order to drain a flooded island. Ted looked down to the ground level where he could see rows of identical, authoritarian men shaking their heads in utter disapproval. They were very unhappy with Ted, but Ted didn't understand why.

"Hey," the woman next to him said. "I told you not to look down."

She stabbed Ted in the neck. He lost his footing and began to fall several stories down before abruptly waking up in his bed.

Ted just finished reliving a dream he had back in 2014.

The thing about unpredictable time travel, if one's consciousness is hopping back and forth, one never knows whether they will be entering into the mind of their sleeping selves or not.

· · · ● · ● ● · ·

"Ted!" Mr. Satin shouted.

Ted was back in 2016, with Mr. Satin scowling next to him.

"You can't just check out when you see fit!" Mr. Satin continued, "Tell me where the fuck you are—"

· · · ● · ● ● · ·

Ted was on the floor of a restaurant called Nark Nark Burgers.

### Nark Nark Burgers: 5 / 5 stars

*It had urinals where the flush handles are covered in dick-sweat condensation. I walked into this bathroom long enough to discover that a trashed visitor of this beautiful club had vomited in a plugged toilet, which was overflowing across the bathroom floor. And his knees.*

*I think he wasn't happy.*
*I was in heaven.*

— Reviewed by *MikeMan*

Ted recognized Mike's voice, saying, "He's alright, just give him space. This happens all the time. He was wounded in Afghanistan, got a silver star for that shit."

A stranger's voice responded. "Really? Damn. Hey, meals on me for those two. Fuckin' war hero and his best friend."

"Thanks, man," Mike said. "Appreciate it. Oh, you back?"

"Yeah," Ted said, crawling back into his chair. "When did we come to Nark Nark?"

"Seriously? Shit." Mike said, taking a moment to take a bite out of his burger before continuing, "No wonder you were so quiet. You just went on autopilot and had a craving for burgers."

It was true that Ted stopped speaking. It was not true that he craved burgers. Mike did.

"How long was I out?" Ted asked.

"You went full-on gone for like a solid ten minutes." Mike said, food falling out of his mouth, "Just fell out of your chair."

"And you left me on the ground?" Ted asked.

Mike stopped eating, stared at Ted, and said, "I heard you're not supposed to move people when things like that happen."

"Great," Ted said, still dazed. "Well, things just got weirder. That guy I keep seeing, his name is Mr. Satin, and—"

A heavy hand landed on Ted's shoulder, and a voice said, "Thank you for serving. We appreciate what you've given for us. Not everybody makes such a sacrifice."

"Uh, yeah." Ted said, his face flush red, "No problem."

Ted glared at Mike. Mike didn't notice, as he was too invested in his free beer and burger.

The man's drunkenness began to show in the way he was swaying. "I just want you to know that some of us actually care."

"Hey," Mike said to the drunk, "can you let us eat? I don't know how much time we have before he falls down again. Let us enjoy this. He has flashbacks every time he drops, so it's not a pleasant ride."

Technically, Mike was right. They were flashbacks, in a way, and many of his trips were unpleasant.

"Oh yes, oh yes, oh yes. Of course, yes, yes." The man continued talking as he walked away, taking his seat at the bar. "Yes, yes. Man. Yes, of course. God, yes! God. Can't imagine."

"Mike," Ted said, "you know you are a total asshole, right?"

Mike acknowledged the statement with a laugh, and some chewed-up burger spilled out of his mouth and onto the table.

• • • • • • • • •

On the way home, walking the streets of Minneapolis, Ted was afraid that he might fall at any moment. To avoid injury, Mike helped him walk around, like he was assisting his drunk friend home. They made it to Ted's place without any problems.

Once Ted walked through the door, relieved, he started to feel a tingling in the back of his head. It was another travel experience. Before he could say a word, he fell to the floor, scraping his chin on the coffee table on the way down.

Ted woke up with Mike kneeling over him.

"You good?" Mike said.

"No."

"What happened?"

"I traveled to some time I was living with my parents, and just woke up from a nightmare. I was just staring at the wall for hours. Once I finally got myself out of bed, I woke up back here."

"Fine, but just look at this shit." Mike placed a newspaper in front of Ted.

Ted looked at it. "Hunting season is approaching?"

"No, not that article. Look at the police reports."

**July 7**
*A hot ATV muffler started a vegetation fire at the site on Kost Dam Road, in Sunrise Township... reported about 11 a.m. No firefighter aid needed, fire was put out by those on-site.*

**July 8**
*Report of somebody shot with a crossbow in Friesland neighborhood in Wyoming shortly after midnight. Lakes Area officers went to help locate suspect who was eventually arrested in North Branch.*

Wyoming is a small town in Minnesota, neighboring other small towns like Lindstrom and Chisago City. Many people in the state aren't aware that the town exists, even those having lived in the state for their entire lives. Much of the world would yet to be introduced to Wyoming by a captioned photo that was to go viral on April 20, 2017—a 4/20 joke, in which an officer holding a fishing net stood near Cheetos set out as a trap:

*Undercover 4/20 operations are in place...*

At this moment in time, in the summer of 2016, it was a small rural town that revealed Ted had had a real-life premonition. He stared in disbelief at the police report, looking back up at Mike.

"Right?! Right?!" Mike repeated. He was giddy with excitement. "You can predict the future, man!"

Ted sat in a pool of confusion, awe, and anxiety that welled up within himself. If he could see something that hadn't happened yet, that really was to come true... how many of his visions of childhood and infant life were spot on? What about the wild, surreal stuff he had seen? Was that imagery a distorted vision of the truth?

Could he interpret these images like one might do with a dream, taking it apart to reveal something more about oneself or maybe the future?

Ted said, "Well, even if I knew it was the future, it's not like I could stop it. I couldn't tell where it was, when it was going to be, and if it was actually going to happen. All I had to go on was a truck in the distance, with no license plate, and a dude named Dick shooting another dude with a crossbow."

"You saw something happen, not far off in the future, in Wyoming—nearby."

"Right."

"Maybe this is like your powers starting to develop."

"No."

"No?"

"It could just be the extent of what I can do. It feels useless. The rest of the time, I'm just tripping out in my own past."

"You serious? I can't believe you right now, but hey, I have an interview," Mike said, continuing to talk as he walked into the bathroom. "So I gotta go. But if you have any more anything, make sure to write it down somewhere. Maybe shout at your phone to take auto-dictation if I'm not around. Makes it easier to revisit."

Mike stepped out of the bathroom wearing a dress shirt and slacks. He threw a box at Ted.

"Where did this come from?"

"Your mom."

It really did.

Mike, looking at himself in a mirror near the entryway, said, "Wish me luck with this dumb shit."

With a nervous smile, Ted responded, "Good luck."

Opening the box, Ted found a Vikings football helmet. He put it on and sat alone in his apartment.

## Beertopia: 3 / 5 stars

*You need a door code to get into the bathroom here.*

*I asked the bartender for the code, but her attractive, radiant smile stalled my language capabilities.*
*"Code of bathroom," I said.*
*"12345. Then hashtag."*
*"Hashtag, no. I call it pound. 12345 pound it."*

*The bathrooms are single stall, and gender-neutral. Toilet paper was stuffed into the porcelain-bowl swallowing hole, which I should have taken as a red flag. A big, shitty red flag. But I ignored it.*
*So. Fire in the hole.*

*But it wouldn't flush. I wielded the goddamn plunger of the gods, to no avail. The swirling, foggy pool only took on more water. It was starting to bubble over the ledge. Why the fuck did I eat corn today? I tried for another 15 minutes before running out of the bathroom and closing my tab.*
*It wasn't me. Someone else sabotaged me.*

*They had 35 beers on tap.*
*I had a brown ale made with cacao nibs.*

— Reviewed by *MikeMan*

# 7

## WORK LIFE

Mike landed the job. It was at a distribution warehouse for Lucidon, an online-shopping giant. Initially starting as an online record store in the '90s, they evolved into an everything store. Member$Mart was the bulk, member-only wholesale landing zone, whereas Lucidon was for those who never wanted to leave their houses.

On his first break, Mike was thinking about Dick shooting a crossbow. It reminded him of the Bush administration. Dick Cheney, as a previous vice president of the United States, had left quite a legacy. Someone pulling a Dick can mean they are jerking off, but it can also mean accidentally shooting someone in the face.

It should also be noted that when someone is shooting clay pigeons, for hunting practice or sport, they shout out the word "pull."

While thinking of Dick Cheney, Mike overheard a woman in her twenties saying that she wanted to die young, "so that I'm at my most beautiful, right?"

Her name was Cassandra. She followed this up with a paraphrasing that she didn't realize had roots going as far back as the '40s: "Live fast, die young, and leave a beautiful corpse."

Four months later, after another fun blackout drinking night, Cassandra's body would be found as a victim in a murder-suicide. It would take three weeks before her body was identified. She would have been very disappointed to know that she was to have a closed-casket funeral. In all truth, her ex-boyfriend was only wanting to kill himself but had accidentally pulled a Dick when slipping in her vomit.

He was intending to shoot something else: himself.

His only recourse was to follow an age-old proverb popularized by William Edward Hickson in the 1800s:

> *'Tis a lesson you should heed:*
> *Try, try, try again.*
> *If at first you don't succeed,*
> *Try, try, try again.*

Mike was alive and well, annoyed by what he heard in his eavesdropping but still happily eating ice cream. The local ice cream shop had a flavor of the week called Praline 'N Cream. Praline has its origins in France, where the confection is made of almonds and caramelized sugar. It was brought over to the United States where chefs substituted the almonds for pecans, due to the abundance of pecan trees.

A Southern twang pronounces pecan as "pih-(wrath of)-kahn." Others say "pee-can." Perhaps even "pee-(wrath of)-kahn."

Out of the respect for Southern tradition, and the editor's suggestion, please read it as it was meant to be: *Pih-kahn.*

Human language is quite beautiful. Very flowery. Many weeds in the garden. Some people hate dandelions, and others drink dandelion tea. Did you know that there is at least one pun in this entire novel? Bet you didn't. Don't worry, this book is written with an attention deficit disordered audience in mind.

Approximately 6.4 million kids have been treated for ADD, along with many more adults.

The Narrator has chosen a very good, niche audience with a book that bounces around like a free mobile app full of advertisements.[1]

One might wonder what is so special about pralines. The description of the ice cream claimed that this deliciousness was as much a staple of the South as fried chicken, grits, the Kentucky Derby, mint juleps, Confederate flags, and barbecue ribs. The ice cream parlor, laughably and unknowingly, used the following as a sales pitch:

Taste some South in your mouth!

Sales of the frozen dessert were less than ideal.

Mike ordered it immediately upon reading the pitch.

• • • • • • • •

Mike wasn't the only one working. Ted felt that he needed to leave the house and, with the help of his social worker, landed a good gig back at Member$Mart.

One could say he was very Member-smart about that.

Please don't stop reading the story because of the above line. Fun activity: Cross out the words you don't like when you read them. Use a sharpie. Make poetry. Really bad poetry. If this is being read

---

1. *Disclaimer: Proceeds from every purchase of this book will result in prayer-power toward Dr. Simon Kant's well-being. Godspeed.*

on a digital device, then it's time to go through the stages of grief until you reach acceptance.

Around the time Mike was getting some South in his mouth, Ted was eating another Polish sausage. He found it hard to avoid such a good deal. His helmet had become a safeguard when moving around, only being taken off when he'd eat.

Goose was tending the gas station that day and was sitting with Ted during his break. His nickname came from his frustrations at all the Canada geese that would wander around in front of the gas pumps. He was in his sixties and suffered greatly from irritable old man syndrome.

Ted didn't know his real name, even though the man wore his name tag in plain view each day. He was wearing it right then. Ted's brain continued its habit of blocking it out, a pre-concussion mental affliction.

"Ted, those damn geese are out there again. Honkin' an' shittin'. That's all they do."

"Oh?"

"Sometimes I run at 'em."

"You do?"

"Damn right I do! They hiss like feral cats and scatter."

"Do you have to do it often?"

"Every day. Members can't fill up their gas unless I do it. I wouldn't doubt those geese have the balls to walk into oncoming traffic. They think they're untouchable."

"I bet."

Ted ran into the same woes when he would wander outside to collect shopping carts, back when he didn't have to wear a helmet when mobile. The geese felt entitled to the parking lot, though they were open to debate.

"If I could," Goose said, "I'd throw on my blaze-orange vest and go open season on 'em with my twelve-gauge and some buckshot. You ever eat geese, Ted?"

"No, sir."

"Don't call me sir."

"Okay."

"Well, I'll say this about eating geese. It only tastes good if you're the one to blow them out of the sky. I hope one day you get to experience the feeling of eating and not knowing whether you're about to crack a tooth on a metal bead of buckshot."

Ted cringed slightly at the thought, imagined the taste of iron float across his tongue, and felt a traveling event approaching.

"I need to go," Ted said.

Part of his deal was a private cot in a converted cubicle, just a few steps into the main office. He plopped his helmet on and rushed over.

He had the process down.

This time he was able to get his helmet off and rest his head on a pillow.

• • • ● • ● • • •

As he drifted, the fluorescent lights flickered around him. He drifted into a time when he was on a train, reading a book. The passing of trees strobe-lit the pages, making it difficult to see the text.

The book was Bluespeaking: Bluetooth as Societal Placebo for Schizophrenia. The inner flap of the cover said, in big, important-looking words.

## A STUDY OF SCHIZOPHRENIC ASSIMILATION VIA ACTS OF SOCIAL NORMALCY

The author had used a similar tactic to that of your humble, extremely beautiful Narrator. At the top of the page that Ted was reading, right-aligned and italic, was an opening quote:

> *"When acting truly sane, in a society where madness is the norm, you'll undoubtedly be perceived as out of your mind."*
>
> Unknown

This was a sign that Ted was reading a very good book, written by a well-studied intellectual. The wisdom of the author was surely set. A more gifted author would also have added:

> *"Unknown" is the most quoted entity of all time.*
>
> Unknown

Fun fact: In the English language, you cannot spell authority without author. See? More evidence.

You should feel powerless, as a mere reader. Why? Another obvious and fun fact: In the English language, you cannot spell dread without read. See? Further proof you are weak and should fear The Narrator's gift of the written word.

The central hypothesis of the book that Ted was reading was that someone having verbal discussions with voices would become less obtrusive due to the explosion of the adoption of Bluetooth technology. Many people were mistaken as either speaking to themselves, or someone nearby, to the point that it had become acceptable for an individual to appear to be speaking to someone on the phone.

This theory was never really evaluated, and the book had sold very few copies. The handful of psychiatrists who believed a headset could work as a placebo treatment were surprised at how awful the results were. How were they fooled by such a ridiculous notion?

Anybody can write a book.

Anybody can wield the power of written text.

The Onion is often mistaken as an actual news source.

What wasn't clear about the book was that the author had written an exhausting satire that only he found hilarious. Because it was written in such a professional fashion, he was the only one who had understood the joke.

His pen name was Dr. Ayn Al Phissure. Those who would read his book missed that his pseudonym was a phonetic joke. The year of the publication of Bluespeaking, Dr. Phissure—a false name for a false doctor, a misunderstood comedian—was dismissed as a quack. Walks like a duck, acts like a duck. Must be a duck.

Quack.

Remarkably, not one person was to pull a Dick upon seeing that author in public. A schizophrenic treated with the Bluespeaking placebo, however, ran a potential risk of pulling many a Dick. Ted was woefully unaware of this, along with many other people in the world now, despite there being a viral video of evidence.

A viral video is a streamable film that is shared and commented on by a large number of people online. They are unhealthy and distracting things, really. This is quite clearly how the term came to be coined in this way. These commonly break out on YouTube.

YouTube is not a dick joke, even if it is a reference to the "boob tube"—television. YouTube is just the egocentric form of video, online, where anyone can upload their talking head just like the people on cable.

A viral video is also not to be considered the STI of YouTube.[2]

In this case, this infection of a news story was about a man who had been pinned between two vehicles by a person who had gone completely nuts. Right before the driver caused the collision, the madman had picked up a hitchhiker. The hitchhiker was told by the driver that a revelation had just struck him.

"I'm God. I can do anything!" the driver shouted.

Many people think they are God. Life would potentially be easier if everyone accepted a polytheistic doctrine like Hinduism.

After the car crash, the driver got out of the car and started beating a hysterical woman who witnessed the occurrence. The hitchhiker rose to the occasion, pulled out an axe from his trusty backpack, and cracked the crazy guy's head open. The God-claiming man, all 6'4" and 280 pounds of bleeding divinity, stumbled away from the scene toward an elementary school.

The hitchhiker was a hero of the internet.

The driver was found by police. He was all alone, indecently exposed, and pulling a Dick on school grounds.

No shotgun was involved. Metaphorically, though, there was.

---

2. *The target readership of this book is disgusting.*

# NOSTALGIA

*Onanism* is a Biblical term for *masturbation*, which can also mean using the withdrawal method during sex. A man named Onan had withdrawn during sex with his brother's widow, and God killed him for doing so. The church points to this tale to explain why it abhors birth control, contraceptives, and touching thyself.

"Oh, man! Onan!"
A person witnessing Onan's death in Biblical times

What the public was unaware of, in regard to the viral video, was that the man had been treated by Dr. Simon Kant. The patient was treated with a Bluespeaking placebo and had been wearing a Bluetooth headset on his right ear. Imagine that! The accident of holy revelation was caused by a relapse of being off medication.

Quack quack quack.

Quack.

The evening of that event "going viral" online, Dr. Simon Kant's night terrors had a notably higher number of demons struggling with their can openers. He tried to teach them the ways of humans and their black magic of de-canning. One demon became so frustrated that, out of hunger, it shoved an incorrectly opened can into its misshapen face. The sharp rim of the can split its upper lip open. It let out dark, deep, shivering screams. Much blame and shame was thrown at the psychiatrist, by the whole mob of them.

Upon waking, with his years of education and knowledge of psychoanalysis, he had committed an act of dream interpretation:

He needed to pray harder.

He needed to *try, try, try again.*

# 8

## BIOHACKING VS. NARCOLEPSY

Ted's social worker was going to drive him to his group meetings, because Ted was a hazard to himself and others on the road. By this point, Ted had two groups on his list: the Narcolepsy Network and the Biohackers group. The first one up?

"You want me to drive you to these Biohacker people?" Cheryl said.

Cheryl was Ted's temporary social worker, acting as a chauffeur into the world of waking life. She helped him get back to work. Ted sat in the back seat of her car, his football helmet under his arm.

"Yes," he said. "They focus on diet, exercise, and sleep stuff. At least, that's what I've heard. Bleeding edge. Maybe."

Ted was a little concerned. He had no idea who was going to be attending tonight. People who made specialized coffee, others who would micro-dose psilocybin, and there were people who embedded hardware under the skin in an attempt to become like cyborgs.

He never knew there were real cyborgs; yet, here they were.

"Your doctor recommended this?" Cheryl said.

She had heard of the group and had been notified that there was a risk of pseudo-science activity around neural feedback loops. Another social worker had been upset when she found that one of her clients had been persuaded into spending $15,000 on a one-week boot camp program. Biohackers had even assisted the woman in obtaining a personal loan at a specialized banking office.

Ted assured her that Dr. Simon Kant had indeed recommended the group.

The meeting was at a workout-themed café, in a back room. Ted sat down, his football helmet limiting his view into tunnel vision, and waited for it to begin. Some people were chatting about the differences they found when micro-dosing psilocybin and LSD, others about stoicism, and then there was the dominating subject of the day:

Injecting your own blood into your gonads.

"For awareness," the head organizer, Moon, continued, "this was invented by the same doctor that made the vampire facial."

Moon smiled. The group reflected her smile, showed awe, and gave nods of approval.

At that point, Ted worried he had stumbled onto a cult. He took his helmet off, allowing his head to breathe. He hadn't heard of a vampire facial before and asked about it. A mix of disbelief and excitement came from those around him. Moon brought up a YouTube video of a woman with microneedles punching holes in her face.

Moon narrated. "They are using PRP—platelet-rich plasma—instead of straight-up blood here, and the doctor is punching holes into her face."

Another person present chimed in excitedly. "A few of us have set up our own centrifuge systems at home so that we can draw our own blood and extract the plasma. We hacked together fidget spinners at the local makerspace, and now we—"

"I believe I must leave now," Ted said.

"Oh, already?"

"Yes." Ted took out his phone, pretending to look at something that was demanding his attention. His phone was dead, so he just stared at the blank screen.

"Ah," he said, "that's right. Forgot about that. It was nice meeting everybody."

"We'll post resource links online so that you can learn about the sexual benefits the injections have."

"Thank you. Looking forward to it."

Nobody asked questions when he put his helmet back on. Their curiosity seemed to be directed to the theme of the day. Ted began walking casually toward the exit before he collapsed and struck his helmet against a female attendee.

• • • • • • • • •

He traveled to his high-school years and found himself giving a presentation about a man named Chase Trenton Richardson.

"Also known as the Vampire of Santa Monica," he said.

Chase was a long-time drug abuser in the '70s and was in a deepening state of drug-induced psychosis. There were many warning signs of this man being on the road to hell. He had been found in the woods one night, naked and covered in pig's blood.

Chase's mother caught him tearing a cat apart and rubbing the entrails all over his face.

He once ran into a hospital in fear that his skull was growing at such a fast rate that it was splitting the skin of his face open.

His conclusion, eventually, was that his problems were derived from a secret disease which involved his blood turning into powder. After attempting to inject himself with blood from a rabbit and nearly dying of blood poisoning, he realized that he had been mistaken about the key to his survival.

He needed human blood.

He murdered six randomly chosen people in the span of a month, including a baby whose remains were partially discarded in a Chinese takeout box. The head was found behind a church.

Ted received hesitant applause from his high-school peers when he finished.

Mr. Satin was sitting on the teacher's desk. He laughed, applauded loudly, and howled with satisfaction.

· · · • · • · · ·

Ted woke up. The woman he had hit had stuffed her nose with pieces of tissue that were now stained red.

In contrast to his expectation that people might have called an ambulance, or might ask Ted about his state of health, the meeting had continued. Someone had brought a projector which was playing some kind of news special. It showed a journalist sitting in direct view of another woman's splayed legs. It was a patient waiting for an injection.

"Your vagina looks like mine," the journalist said.

The patient, sounding relieved, said, "Oh, that's good to hear. I always worried about that."

They both nervously laughed, and the doctor played with a syringe of blood.

# NOSTALGIA

Ted stood up quietly and left, unnoticed.

Cheryl wanted to hear how it went.

"You were right. Those people are losing their minds," Ted said.

Saying this out loud, he realized how completely disconnected from reality his everyday routine was becoming. Even though he was working hard to maintain his grip navigating his new life, he had seen people completely lost and without a neurological disorder wrecking their reality.

It was almost voluntary.

Cheryl sighed, shook her head, and drove him home.

• • • ● • ● • • ·

Narcolepsy can be extremely debilitating, and it affects about one in every two thousand people.

"You should count your stars, Ted, that you don't have astasia!" Dr. Simon Kant was manically expressive today. "You really should join the Narcolepsy Network. I think you wouldn't feel so alone in all of this."

He handed Ted a card with a symbol that looked like a sleepy yin-yang. It was the symbol of the Narcolepsy Network. Written on it was the name of a local chapter organizer.

"Sharon Liles," Ted said.

"Yes, Sharon does a great job putting all of it together. You should reach out and attend sometime."

Ted did, thanks to his superhero social worker Cheryl.

Ted was late, walking into a café tucked in the back of a clinic while a woman was starting to tell a story of a recent experience. She talked about waking up on the back of a killer whale in the middle of the sea, finding herself face down just above the surface of the water. Terrified, she had a cataplexic collapse before her surroundings faded away to become her familiar bedroom.

Ted spoke up, "I'm new. I'm Ted. I was wondering—"

The group responded. "Hey Ted!"

"Yeah," Ted continued, "thanks. You said *cataplexy?*"

"I'm Sharon. You've had sleep paralysis, right?" she responded.

"Yes."

"Imagine, instead of waking up and finding yourself paralyzed, that you are already awake. Maybe you're on the bus, and you overhear a funny story because you forgot your headphones. Bam! Same feeling of sleep paralysis happens and you slump over. Hopefully you were smart enough to sit down."

"Sounds familiar," Ted said, pointing at his Minnesota Vikings helmet. "This is why I wear this purple helmet everywhere. It's sort of a similar situation."

"At least you're a Vikings fan," someone chimed in.

"Yup!" Ted said, though he had never watched or played football in his entire life.

Throughout the meeting, Ted learned terminology that helped explain his everyday existence.

His dreams that lasted only for a few seconds were called micro-sleeps. When his dreams bled into his waking life, in a half-asleep sort of way, they were called in-between states. There were hypnogogic and hypnopompic, or pre-sleep and post-sleep, hallucinatory states. Cataplexy—called astasia in Dr. Simon Kant's ancient reference book—was when the body fell helplessly to sleep while the individual stayed perfectly conscious. These were often kicked off by emotions as simple as laughter. This was the analogy that Sharon made, about sudden sleep paralysis.

In early documentation of narcolepsy from the 1870s, one man had as many as two hundred micro-sleep episodes a day. In 1928, a twenty-two-year-old found himself briefly paralyzed whenever he woke up, coupled with vivid hallucinations. Later on, sleep paralysis and hallucinations would be known as common symptoms of narcolepsy.

A member of the group told of a pale woman that sat on his chest in a nighttime vision.

"I crawled into bed to get to sleep. I felt my body sink into the mattress, while I was face-up, and then I couldn't move anymore. It was like my body was happy to go to sleep without my mind. Then this woman, her face all distorted and eyes misaligned, calmly sat on my chest. The pressure was becoming immense until she finally slid off, then laid down beside me. She was breathing irregularly into my left ear. I couldn't move," he said.

When the man started to pull himself out of cataplexy, enough to shift his face toward the woman, her eyes were bugging out of her head as she shouted numbers at him.

"Did you..." Ted said, trailing off.

"Did I what?" the speaker asked.

"Did you write down the numbers? Or do you remember what they were?" Ted asked.

The man had written them down in his narcolepsy journal, which, as Ted discovered, many members used as a method of interpreting their own experiences. Ted, fighting a feeling of delusion over the potential meaning of the numbers, resisted asking more questions about it.

One person talked about a children's book which had the sole purpose of teaching about narcolepsy.

"*Sometimes*, the main character of the story says, *I find my socks in the fridge without remembering placing them there.*"

Sleep walking, talking, or simply standing and staring can afflict the narcoleptic via the side effects of medications.

Ted felt his consciousness pull, and he started traveling.

· · · ● · ● · · ·

It was 1989 again, the year of his birth. His mother, Ellen Bundy, believed that reading to a child at any age was a great idea. She was reading a book called *Is Your Mama a Llama?* by Deborah Guarino.

The book had only just been published that year. Another book, *The Dark Half* by Stephen King, was published that year, too. As a teenager, Ted would feel like some aspect of himself was splitting away. He would read King's book in 2005 and be profoundly affected.

In 2005, Ted would reference the llama book of his childhood in an offhand joke, asking a student peer whether his mama was, indeed, a llama. Ted terribly miscalculated the joke by expecting that people would realize he was referencing the nostalgia of childhood nonsense. A fist collided with his face as the boy interpreted the comment as an insult to his mother.

· · ● · ● · ● · · ·

In 1989, Ted patiently waited until the end of his mother's reading. It turns out, many other mamas exist without having to be llamas.

He then spit up all over himself. This was accompanied by the constant opening and closing of Teddy's hands, as a toddler, while he laughed at the absurdity of being alive.

• • • ● • ● • • •

Ted was coming to, back in 2016. At first, he felt embarrassed. Sharon gave him a reassuring smile. A man's voice said, "There's nothing to feel ashamed of," since Ted was surrounded by narcoleptics on all sides. The man followed the comment with a loud, brief laugh before cataplexing into a limp rag doll.

Ted had found his people.

For the first time since he was a little boy, he felt a form of happiness that comes with the understanding and empathy of fellow human beings. His everyday existence wasn't alien to these people; they had terms for his experiences, and they even had espresso-infused cookies. Everyone had a delicious cup of hand-crafted coffee from the café.

Sharon was even drinking some Bulletproof Coffee, but Ted didn't mind. He didn't even bring up people injecting blood into their private parts.

# 9

## FAMILY

Ted didn't get to meet his grandfather, Myron Bundy. The Narrator knows Myron only ever talked about his misfortunes. When doing so, he would often end his statements with *livin' the dream.*

"How's it going, Myron?"

"Oh, you know, the mill dropped me onto the street like a discarded newspaper. Now I'm behind on my bills, and my wife is riding my ass every day about what I'll be doing about it."

"Ouch."

"Livin' the dream."

Myron carried the same straight-faced attitude into his final days of cancer.

"Dad," Luke Bundy said, "the doc says you don't have much longer to go."

Myron shifted his gaze from the ceiling to Luke, and said, "You know me, son."

"Yeah?"

"Livin' the dream."

This manner of observing life was passed down to Luke and was something his son Ted often heard as a young boy.

When Luke stubbed his toe?

"Jesus Christ!"

"What happened?" Ellen asked, concerned.

"Just livin' the dream, livin' the dream," he laughed, then stopped abruptly with a facial expression of vengeance, and punched a hole in the wall. It really had no business being in his way.

Mike's father, Travis Turnkey, was an alcoholic and AWOL parent since Mike was eleven years old. Travis had his own saying, which was just as useful as the traditional Bundy refrain: *ain't life grand?*

This was a case where answering a question could easily be done by responding with another question.

Is there an overdraft penalty on your checking account?

Whoops, does it look like the untouched milk in the fridge has begun to curdle?

Is a hangnail preventing you from walking like a normal human?

One answer to rule them all: Ain't life grand?

Looking at Travis and Luke, these drunkards, some might conclude that two bodies can share the same soul. Einstein said, as a joke about prohibition law, "I don't drink. So it's all the same to me."

He also said, of quantum entanglement, that it was "spooky action at a distance."

One can only imagine what revelations would have occurred to Einstein had he been able to witness Travis Turnkey and Luke Bundy in spooky action.

• • • • • • • •

Travis Turnkey had abandoned the family after he placed all of his money into something he believed the Robert J. Dole Institute of

Politics would covet dearly. It was a Bob Dole doll with an embedded speaker chip that replayed various quotes. The prototype he made only included three memorable sayings in order to save on cost in producing the one-off.

Travis despised Bill Clinton. He told Mike, when Mike was a kid, that the White House had multiple meanings now.

"He defiled it with his pecker, boy, and he's the goddamn President of the United States!" Travis once told Mike.

One of the quotes his prototype doll said, in Bob Dole's authoritative voice, was, "If something happened along the route and you had to leave your children with Bob Dole or Bill Clinton, I think you would probably leave them with Bob Dole."

"Damn right I would!" Travis said, in 2016. There he was, bellied-up to a bar in Reno, with the doll in his hands. He pushed Bob Dole's face with his thumb, pressing the button of the chip inside.

"Life is very important to Americans," Bob Dole's voice said.

"Ain't nothin' truer than that!"

The Robert J. Dole Institute of Politics said that they would not pay for Travis's tribute to Bob. The response letter included a notice that lawyers would pursue legal action against him if he were to manufacture and distribute the "contraption." Two weeks later, a restraining order was also placed against Travis.

Bob Dole never laid eyes on the Bob Dole doll, but one would imagine that he would have said, "I'm Bob Dole, and Bob Dole did not approve or authorize this... abomination."

Travis finished his beer, looked at the bartender, and said, "Ain't life grand?"

"Sure is," the bartender said. "Sure is."

# NOSTALGIA

• • • • • • • • •

Ted was back at work, staring off into the distance, as members made their way in. Carol, the Member$Mart pharmacist, said hello to Ted as she was stepping out for a smoke break.

Ted had drifted into multiple roles at Member$Mart before the accident. One of the roles was as a pharmacy assistant, and he had been enrolled in training to become a pharmacy technician. By law, in order to continue working in the pharmacy, Ted was told he would need to become certified within 60 days of his employment. Narcotics were locked up in a safe, but outside that, he was surrounded by pills in a beautiful range of colors.

Member$Mart members could get special discounts on generic medications.

Ted wasn't aware of the drastic cost difference between generic medications and brand-name versions. For the most part, these medications were exactly the same but the coating differed—and these coatings sometimes caused allergic reactions in patients.

Outside that potential issue, generics were at times the difference between a $5 and $700 prescription. Some patients, so convinced by commercials and smiling actors, believed they needed to get the brand-name version anyway.

Insurance companies were the bane of a pharmacist's existence. Carol had many things to say about them.

"I know someone who has Dupuytren's contracture," she told Ted one day.

"Oh? What's that?"

"Have you heard of the Celtic hand?"

"Sounds like a horror film."

"It's where lumps develop in the hands and extend into the fingers. Eventually, the hand contracts. People end up unable to shake hands or do basic tasks. It's a disease that can be treated but will continue to recur."

"That sucks. I wonder if—"

"What's worse is that insurance companies generally see surgery as cosmetic. That is, until it has progressed enough to cause problems and pain in the hands or feet."

"Feet?"

"Yeah, your feet and toes can start to tighten and curl inward. The insurance companies aren't the issue here, Ted, it's the health system itself. Couple that with blame culture and doctors needing to protect themselves from being sued. Insurance costs blowing up, in addition to the cost of treatment, are some of the effects. Obamacare approached universal health care as an insurance issue, but that's only treating the effects and not the problem."

She stopped filling out a digital form for a member and said something under her breath. Ted didn't hear it. What she was saying was *fuck them all*.

Unknown to Ted, the person Carol knew with the Celtic hand issue was her husband. This caused considerable issues in home life and in work life for both of them. The man was a carpenter.

Jesus, the messiah of Christianity, was a carpenter, too. When he died, it is said that he did quite a bit of remodeling in heaven.

Ted was able to learn many other fun facts while working in the pharmacy. His attention was easily diverted, making pill counting difficult. Unfortunately, he was tasked with counting pills to fill up little orange bottles. There were many recounts in his two months there.

"You realize, with some of these, that you can negatively impact a person's health? By miscounting?" Carol asked him once. She was annoyed by his uncanny ability to become distracted, requiring a recount.

"A *member's* health," Ted said.

"What?"

"A member's health. You said a person's health instead, when you—"

"Oh my God, just shut up."

During an annual presentation, Carol told employees that Viagra was once again the top-selling medication of the year. This was for the fourth year in a row.

Four.

If you take Viagra and an erection lasts more than four hours, seek medical attention immediately. This may sound hilarious, but this condition is serious. Called a *priapism*, a name derived from the Greek god of fertility, Priapus, usually pictured with a massive hard-on. This side effect translates into permanent erectile dysfunction.

Worse, a four-hour chub can result in losing one's member.

A Member$Mart member is still allowed to shop at Member$Mart if he loses said member, though the Bible does unfortunately frown on this predicament when it comes to attending a religious service.

> *He that is wounded in the stones, or hath his privy member cut off, shall not enter into the congregation of the LORD.*
>
> Deuteronomy 23:1, King James Bible

The question *How's it hanging?* can, therefore, be a critical question for a man and his relationship with God. One can imagine synagogues and churches everywhere posting a bouncer at the entrance, asking the question of every male of any age.

One may wonder whether vasectomies are an offense against God, or whether blue balls are also quite appalling to Him. Afflicted individuals should be okay, depending on the translation, as "wounded" can be read as "crushed."

As The Narrator, memberless in my nature, I have made a simple rhyme to help any distressed man in this predicament.

> *Rashed or blue, communion for you.*
> *Flat or crushed, good chances now hushed.*

Some Catholic theologians teach that vasectomies, being a voluntary sterilization, can only be permissible if the person repents to God and never has sexual intercourse with a woman again. That is, unless he is married and she has begun menopause. The alternative is to undergo surgery to reverse the vasectomy.

Dicks aside, the number four has particular relevance in Western society.

If you hate your day job, there is a book called *The 4-Hour Work Week* that explains how you should shut the hell up and take control of your life, you big tool.

If you work a twenty-hour work week in a part-time job, and you embrace the concept of the Pareto principle, then only 20 percent of your work really has an impact. That's four hours of actual impact for every twenty hours spent, you uselessly inefficient human.

Outside Viagra and the repeated presence of four, there was one other item that was always a call for celebration in the pharmacy.

"Butt paste is always in demand," Carol explained, "as long as there are both babies and really sweaty adults."

The butt paste supplied to Member$Mart is labeled with the following tagline: *Kicking rash and taking names!*

A quote features prominently on the packaging:

> *"I swear by butt paste. Talk about game changing!"*
> Butt Paste-using momma

• • • ● • ● • • •

Ted was traveling.

It was 2003. Ted was fourteen, and he's with the rest of an 8th-grade class in Washington, DC. He was shocked to walk past so many homeless people.

The restaurant in which they had eaten lunch was on a street with massive air vents in the concrete ground. A homeless man had wet himself before passing out on top of them, his unconscious body embracing the heat blasting out. The entire block smelled like urine, making the walk outside an unpleasant one.

Ted had grown up in a rural town and hadn't seen a homeless person before. Visiting such an important place out of his school textbooks, he was confused and disappointed at how unimpressive his experience was. The statues of founding fathers literally cast shadows over beggars.

At this moment in traveling, Ted was in the lobby of the hotel that the students and parents were staying at. He had drunk a ridiculous amount of water, and his bladder was screaming for relief. As he attempted to walk to the bathroom, leaving the main group, the chaperone shouted over at him.

"Hey! Nobody move. I'm completely serious. Listen to everything I say before you go off on your own."

Ted froze. The teacher seemed to drone on forever, with absolutely none of it registering with Ted. He was simply waiting for the speech to be over so that he could make his way to the men's restroom.

*Please don't pee, please don't pee,* Ted pleaded with himself.

His insides hurt, and his teeth shuddered.

"Okay," the teacher said, "that is all."

Ted bolted but slowed down when the bathrooms were in sight. Some unconscious part of his brain made the mistake of believing that now that he had sighted his destination, he must already be there. Without his conscious permission, a streak of urine was marking the floor with each footstep. He couldn't stop the flow, and by the time he made it to the urinal, unzipped, and stared... there was nothing left to do. His pants were soaked.

Ted felt a shared humanity with the homeless man, a brotherhood of soiled pants. He wanted to collapse somewhere, pass out, and ignore the world.

• • • • • • • • •

Ted awoke, back in 2016.

He felt like an old man with Alzheimer's, having difficulty understanding when and where he was. Looking around, he noticed a nurse was in the room.

She smiled at Ted and asked, "Did someone have an accident?"

· · · ● · ● · ● · · ·

Ted awoke, again, on the cot at work. He was having travels within travels, dreams within dreams. His accident that the nurse had noticed was when he was still hospitalized after the car crash.

Ted hadn't seen Mr. Satin in a while, or Sara. He wondered whether he really should get off the medication. Was it causing more harm than good? What happened to seeing the future? What happened to having a superpower?

Medication had helped him regain some control in his life, but he was finding that this life wasn't one he really wanted that much.

"Screw it," Ted said.

He flushed his pills down the toilet.

Studies have shown that salmon in the Pacific Northwest contain traces of antidepressants, cocaine, and other drugs in their systems. Even the tap water in multiple cities has been tested to show psychiatric medications have made their way into the supply.

The suspicion is that people are pissing out samples of the drugs they are taking, and water treatment plants aren't able to sift it out. Scientists are uncertain what the long-term drugging of society, voluntarily and involuntarily, will have on the overall health of the people.

Livin' the (drug-induced) dream.

# 10

## Fulfilling Orders

"I don't know how much longer I can take this job," Mike said.

"Didn't you just start this one?" Ted asked.

"Yeah, but you won't believe the shit that happened today."

Mike could sometimes become an extremely animated storyteller. Ted sat up on the couch, leaning forward. Mike was standing, gesturing wildly.

"First off, I start my shift at my usual station. I notice there's already a box there. It has no labeling on the outside. So, I open that shit up just to see what I'm working with. You know what it is?"

Mike stared at Ted anxiously, waiting for a response. At work, Mike had to open large boxes all day, and scan hundreds of items to be sorted later by robots driving around the warehouse.

"Uh, what was it?" Ted asked.

"Dicks, Ted. A big huge box of dicks. And these weren't even dick-size dicks, either. No, these things were forearm-size blunt weapons. Just measure from your elbow to your fingertips, and there you are: a king dick."

Ted's eyes glazed over.

"So," Mike went on, "I tape that box back up."

"You didn't sort it out?"

"I wasn't going to deal with it! The guy before me passed it on for the same reason, probably. Yeah, I tape it back up. I start dealing with all the other boxes that are coming in, the usual bullshit. You wouldn't imagine the stupid things people buy, Ted. It makes me sick. The amount of ridiculous consumption by people. All of it—"

"Mike, what about the dicks, then?"

"Oh yeah. So then my supervisor walks over to chat with me. As we're talking, he motions toward the box, asking what it is. I tell him it was left over by the previous shift. He walks over, tears it open, and he locks up. Just stops in place. His face turns red. He starts laughing and then takes a picture with his phone. He tells me that shit's hilarious, then walks off. I tape the box back up."

"Again?"

"Yeah, again. I'm not dealing with it!"

"Okay."

"Then this girl, hot as hell, walks over. She works a few stations down. She starts talking to me. Asking me how my day is going, what I'm up to, small-talk stuff. But then she asks is it here? Is what here? You know. She was asking about the dicks, Ted! I nod at the box, she walks over, whips out a box cutter, slits it open, and when she looks inside? She has this big grin on her face. Then she takes one out. Look at these things! she says. She holds it like a shotgun, aims everywhere, looks like she's shooting geese. I'm just like, fuckin' Christ! She puts it away and walks off."

"And you tape it up?"

"Obviously. Then these two douchebags walk over. One asks me if I play *Runescape*. Who the hell plays that? He says he loves it. As one of them talks, the other starts shuffling through my boxes until, yup, he gets to the right one. They must've been looking for it. This time, they swing those dicks around like swords and start battling each other. That wasn't even the worst part. Those guys put the dicks back, and before I can tape the box up, this guy from Somalia walks over."

Mike sighs heavily. "He walks over, saying, Ha! What is this? Do you like this? What is this? then picks one up and smacks me on the arm with it like he's swinging a kid's baseball bat! Fucker hurt! They aren't floppy, they're like those hard rubber police batons."

This wasn't the first time Mike had to handle large shipments of sex toys. Being able to order them online, from the comfort of one's house, made it that much easier to avoid the shame of buying in public.

Every now and then, when he saw a box being packed with an academic textbook, he chose to misplace a toy in the box as a gift.

College life can be stressful.

# 11

## KRAV MAGA

A woman ran up to Ted as he sat in his wheelchair at the Member$Mart entrance, bawling her eyes out.

"What's wrong?" Ted asked, frozen and uncomfortable about her blatant expression of emotion.

"He's a killer! He's a killer!"

She ran past Ted, in his wheelchair and Vikings helmet, toward the customer service desk. Franklin, the target locked in the woman's sights, gave Ted the stink eye for having let a customer enter through the door labeled EXIT.

Ted wasn't about to climb out of his wheelchair and risk head-butting a distressed woman.

She grasped at Franklin's hands, but he jerked them away in disgust.

"Please!" she said, tears rolling down her face.

"What exactly," Franklin asked slowly, "happened?"

Goose had finally had the last straw. When he ran at the geese they seemed to mock him, hissing at their challenger. They caught on that he was powerless to do anything to them, and they also learned that vehicles weren't machines of death most of the time. Geese had the right of way in life, as far as they were concerned.

In the middle of changing out the receipt roll in one of the pumps, he caught sight of a goose brazen enough to walk in front of a large SUV. The goose honked, and the vehicle slammed out its own honk in response. Neither of them would give in, a stalemate of honks. The member driving the massive-vehicle-of-gentleness was a woman frantically throwing her arms up at the windshield. She gave piercing and unblinking glares at Member$Mart's lead attendant: Goose.

He looked from the rebellious goose, to the woman, to the weighted receipt roll in his hand. He performed an overhead throw and shouted, "Git!"

The roll nicked the goose's head, and the jerking motion snapped the beast's fragile neck. This resulted in a final quick honk, the limp noodling of its neck, and a slow collapse to the pavement. As far as the distressed woman was concerned, she just witnessed a murder. Goose felt the blood drain from his face, having hoped the roll would simply scare the creature into stepping away.

Instead, Goose had slain one of God's creatures.

"It's dead!" the woman shouted at Franklin. "It's lying in front of my car!"

Ted had only heard about half of this outburst before he drifted elsewhere. He had traveled to a time when he was seven years old, visiting a relative's farm. His cousin, ten years old, was with him. They were near a pond, where they discovered little goslings running around.

A mother goose discovered the boys at the same time.

In a burst of defensive mothering, the goose hissed and ran toward Ted. Screaming at the rage of an animal protecting its young, Ted tried to run. The mother goose wasn't going to give up. Ted's cousin could only laugh and point.

Cornered near a large patch of poison ivy and thorns of blackberries, Ted shifted from flight to fight. He spun around and attempted to scare the goose with a side kick. His foot smacked against its head, mid-hiss, snapping the beast's neck.

His cousin fell silent. Ted Bundy was now a murderer, just like his namesake.

They talked about where to hide the body.

"It will take too long to bury it," his cousin said, "so let's throw it in the pond."

Ted, terrified and on autopilot, nodded in agreement. The two of them picked up the goose as a team, murder having brought them together like nothing before, and they hobbled toward their destination. They counted to three, and swung Ted's victim into the water. Both boys stared in horror as the goose resisted the depths of a watery grave. It floated like a buoy of evidence.

Together, the boys went inside. They were offered ice cream, which they both accepted but couldn't eat. They stirred their ice cream until it became vanilla soup.

Neither boy was ever discovered as having committed the atrocity.

Six happy goslings died shortly after, unable to survive.

The serial killer who was electrocuted in 1989, Ted Bundy, had confessed to thirty murders. Little Teddy, born in 1989, was almost a third of his way there at age seven. He had already claimed an entire family. God was surely writing this down in his book of sins.

Santa may have taken notice, too, if he wasn't tripping balls on reindeer piss.

Ted traveled back to the present, back at Member$Mart in his helmet and wheelchair. He witnessed his manager telling Goose that he was suspended from work without pay. The witness who had reported him watched this interaction, arms crossed, as he hung his head in shame.

Ted was wiping some drool from his mouth when he noticed the member approaching him again.

"Hello," she said. "Remember how I was just here to report what happened to that poor goose?"

"Um, yes."

"Can you get someone to come out and move the poor body somewhere, so I can fill my gas tank?"

"Sure."

"Can you tell me when it's done? I don't want to see it."

"I will."

"Good."

• • • • • • • • • •

Throat strike.

Kick to the balls.

Eye gouge.

What these have in common is Krav Maga and Laura Hitchens. Ted was an ex-boyfriend, but she didn't take shit. She left him because of his complete lack of drive.

Once, when Laura was still dating Ted, a friend of hers asked what Ted's interests were. What were his life goals? Anything interesting?

Laura was horrified to find she had difficulty answering the question.

The moment she saw Ted again, she needed to ask. She needed to know, and she felt embarrassed that she didn't know already.

"Ted," she said, "we haven't talked about it much, but what are your interests? Like, what do you see yourself doing in the future?"

"My interests?" Ted repeated. He couldn't maintain eye contact. He just stared at the wall behind her, saying, "Nothing really. I have no interests, I guess. I like playing video games?"

That was how he met Mike. It wasn't in the physical world—no, it was in the digital.

"No interests?" Laura said.

"Nope."

Laura was overwhelmed with the realization that she needed to leave Ted because he was incredibly unremarkable as a human being.

"Nothing?" she said.

"Yup, nothing," Ted said. "I just live the life, I guess."

It always irritated Laura when he said "I guess," as though he wasn't even in touch with his own thoughts.

"I'm leaving you," she said.

"You're what?"

"I'm breaking up with you."

"Why?"

"You literally just said you have no interests! None! What the hell do you think about or do in your free time, other than waste time?"

Ted had no answer. He was trying to fathom what was happening.

"I guess—"

"You guess?! The fuck, Ted! Really?!"

Laura grabbed her stuff, thanked herself for never having moved in with Ted, and went to the door.

"Wait!" Ted said.

She stopped and glared at him.

Slowly, Ted opened his mouth, but no words came out.

"Yes?" she said.

"Uh, you have my second pair of keys, you know."

Carl, Ted's tabby cat, was in freak-out mode due to all the energy in the room. I know, I said I wouldn't mention this cat again, but Carl bolts into action when he is ignored for too long. Laura had taken the spare key off her chain and threw it at Ted. Carl leaped, with his claws fully extended, at Ted's torso.

Ted screamed.

Laura screamed.

Laura left, never to enter Ted's life again.

· · · • · • · · ·

Laura had been afraid of guns since she was thirteen years old. Her mom moved due to relationships more often than jobs, usually moving in with men she met over the internet. Along for the ride, Laura joined new schools and whichever church her mom's male interest attended.

At thirteen, they were living in Arizona and attending the Holy Cross Church in Prescott.

In the middle of a church service on a Sunday morning in November, the congregation was standing in song. Matt was unusually tense, and his voice cracked when he tried to sing. He ended up singing in a quiet whisper.

A man entered from outside and walked casually down the center aisle. Laura saw him stop beside a known doctor standing with his family. The doctor, named Hal Williams, had opened an abortion clinic in town. Whenever Matt saw the doctor, he'd mutter something about Hal "killing defenseless babies."

Hal looked at the stranger over his shoulder, and Laura watched him get shot in the face.

The shooter spun around and ran outside.

People were frightened at first. Laura's hand was gripped tightly by her crying mother. Unable to process what was happening, Laura was pale and silent. She would never forget seeing a man's head jolt backward as his body collapsed.

Matt looked Laura in the eyes, directly after the shooting, and said, "It was meant to be." He was sweating, his face red. The shooter was never identified. No arrests were made.

Laura always had a suspicion that Matt was directly linked to the murder. She hated religion and guns, and she especially hated Matt. Outside of being an asshole to her and her mother, he often cited the Bible as proof for his prejudices.

"God talks about slavery in the Bible," he told Laura once, "yet, today, people think they can just go against God."

Her mother was a notoriously terrible judge of character.

The overall mood of the congregation, immediately after the shooting, transitioned to a seeming agreement of "accepting God's will." Reporters came by in the aftermath to ask how people felt about the shooting.

*"Well, I don't agree with what he did, but that doctor had it coming with what he was doing."*

Churchgoer I

*"It was terrible. He shouldn't have died, but we all answer to God for our actions."*

Church Deacon

*"It's karma. He really thought he could just stand in church like that? After killing the innocent?"*

Churchgoer II

Four years later, in New York, a twenty-six-year-old was being overthrown by his suicidal thoughts. He grabbed a .22 pistol and walked into a church service. The Catholic priest giving the sermon was pacing and loudly proclaiming verse, a Bible in his left hand.

The armed young man walked right down the center aisle, fifteen feet from the priest, and fired. Pages shot out of the Bible in what looked like a billow of powder. Everybody froze.

Later, most attendees would say they thought it was part of a skit. They thought confetti had shot out of the book as some sort of metaphor. This interpretation, which people held only for a moment, was quickly dismissed after the shooter fired a second time and blood sprayed out of the priest's neck.

The shooter was disarmed and tackled by two military men who were on leave and at home with their families.

It was discovered that the Catholic priest had molested the young man when he was a child, along with many others, but had been moved from church to church each time complaints were raised. When the boy grew up, he decided he would kill the priest as part of his own suicide.

Both men lived.

The priest now gives sermons in Rhode Island.

# 12

## PLAYING GAMES

*Felony and Misdemeanors* (*F&M*) is a popular video game in which you run around with every weapon imaginable, with the goal of creating mischief in a city of criminals and radical police, throwing the world into chaos. The media regularly attacked the game, in which players could fight, maim, shoot, and run over police officers or random innocents.

The game's "sandbox" approach was responsible for it blowing up when it came to sales. Every new version of the game broke previous records. The newest version, *F&M4: Russian Hammer*, was expected to do so once again.

Megan was waiting in line for this game on release night, in front of a store directly across from a bar. Drunks slunk away from the bar when it closed at 11 p.m., one hour before the game store—Funco Land—was due to open. The boozed-up crowd mocked the wide age range of individuals standing in line for the latest game.

"You guys are just a bunch of stupid nerds!" one said.

"Shut up, asshole!" said a man near the front of the line.

"Oh yeah? What you gonna do, you little shit?"

"Just fuck off."

The drunk tensed up, then jolted his arm forward. He had a knife and stabbed the nerd several times. Nobody else moved. The victim fell to the ground while the knife-wielding man ran off.

"Whoa," one guy in line said, "that was fucking amazing!"

People laughed or breathed sighs of relief. Everybody had pushed themselves into a state of denial, believing that the stabbing was staged as a publicity stunt for the release of the game. The victim walked home, and as an apparent act of revenge, armed himself with a kitchen knife.

At this point, the police met him at his front door. Several pedestrians had seen him bleeding at the front door to his apartment complex, struggling to find his keys.

By 4 a.m., Megan had unlocked six achievement badges in *F&M4*. One achievement was for stabbing her first stranger to death.

• • • ● • ● • • •

"Is she still playing that game?" Ted asked.

"Probably. Nothing wrong with that. I get to sleep on your couch and don't have to hear gunshots from a TV speaker," Mike said.

He also didn't have to fight the temptation to play.

Ted felt a tingling in the back of his head.

"Okay. Whoa. Yup. I'm traveling."

"Look at that. You're still conscious."

"Yeah."

"Sounds like the meds were fucking with you. Who would have thought? Oh, right. Me."

Ted was looking at the crowded parking lot of a Goodwill. A van pulled up, parked, and the driver killed the engine.

"Hey, I think this might be a future thing. I'm in a Goodwill parking lot."

"Which one?" Mike asked.

"I'm not sure."

Ted heard Sara's voice behind him, saying, "I thought you were gone."

He looked over at her. She pointed at the van that had just pulled up. A woman opened the passenger-side door and walked around the front, opening the driver's door.

Mr. Satin stepped out.

"This hasn't happened yet," Sara said to Ted, "but it will. He is going tomorrow."

"He makes a point of going to Goodwill?"

She pointed at the van again. The woman with Mr. Satin now held a basket of clothing. Ted found himself next to her, peering down. It was women's clothing.

The dress on top had a small stain.

Mr. Satin walked toward the store.

"Don't worry, Sophia," he said to her. "You don't want anything from the old you, do you?"

Sophia didn't respond.

Ted snapped away from Goodwill and found himself near a kitchen table. A woman was lying down on the table.

Mr. Satin stood next to it.

In his hand was an icepick, dripping blood. Women lined the walls of the kitchen on all sides. Their faces had no features, no eyes, no mouths. They were mannequins populating a nightmare.

Mr. Satin looked up at the ceiling and exhaled deeply. He wasn't wearing his glasses. His pupils were a faded white, and the surrounding skin was marked with long-healed scar tissue.

"Hello, Ted," Mr. Satin said. He was blocking Ted's view of the table by standing in front of it, but then stepped away to reveal Sophia.

She had a line of blood dripping from her left eye.

"Colorful, isn't it?"

"Is this a nightmare?"

• • • ● • ● • • •

Ted snapped back to the Goodwill parking lot, where Sara stood with her arms crossed.

"Sara, I just saw Mr. Satin with bloody hands and Sophia laid out on a table."

"Yes."

"I don't know what part of this is a nightmare, or a memory, or the future."

"Sophia on the table was the past. This, here, is the Goodwill in Eagan. Come here tomorrow."

Ted felt the pavement beneath his feet tilt sideways. His stomach churned with motion sickness. He felt pressure squeezing his eyes, trying to grasp the convoluted jumps in space, time, and consciousness.

· • • ● • ● • • ·

Ted woke up.

His head was resting on a pillow.

"You stopped mid-sentence when you were talking about a van at Goodwill. You shouldn't get rid of your helmet just yet."

Ted's waking life wasn't stirring, moving, or shaking. It was still. A wall of apathy was falling down, the Berlin Wall separating Ted from meaning, and it was crumbling as though it was the year he was born: 1989.

"Mike, I know what we need to do."

## 13

## SHE SAW, SHE CONQUERED, SHE CAME

Laura was sitting with her friend Wendy in *BoJak's Tavern*.
Today, there wasn't a single plugged toilet in the place. All four were functioning well.

"And so now, I don't care," Laura said, finishing off her chicken wings. "I make tacos the way I want all the time. It's nonstop taco night some weeks."

Wendy laughed, but she cut herself short. Over Laura's shoulder, Wendy recognized the man who had just walked into the bar. This man was James Stratton.

Laura looked back at him, then asked Wendy, "Know him?"

"He's the guy," Wendy said. "That's James."

She looked down, wiping her face with her arm.

"Fuck him," Laura said. "We can leave."

"Then we'd have to pass him."

"Yeah. Do you know the guy with him? Would James start any shit with that other guy there?"

Wendy looked at the other man. He was wearing a cross necklace. It was Johnathan Jesus Christ. In the flesh. In the blood. In the spirit. Forever and ever. Amen.

"I don't know," she said.

"Don't worry. I'm with you. They can fuck right off," Laura said, standing up. "You lead. I'm right behind you. If anything happens, I'm right here."

Trembling, Wendy got to her feet. She took each step like bear traps littered the way out.

Step by step by step.

Until she opened the door with one hand, holding Laura's hand with the other.

James did a double-take. He stomped after her.

Johnathan watched, shouting, "James!" and made it out to the sidewalk.

"Wendy, you dumb bitch," James said.

Wendy looked back. "Get away from me!"

"I'm not fucking leaving," James said. He stepped forward, reaching out to Wendy and trying to move past Laura. This was when years of training slipped her into autopilot.

The fist at the end of Laura's left arm crashed into his throat. The knuckles of her right followed up into his face.

It was a very quick introduction.

First impressions are very important. Anyone who knows business will tell you this.

Handshakes.

Hugs.

Fist fights.

They all leave an impression that people remember.

Johnathan Jesus Christ wanted to come to his disciple's aid. This can be very problematic for a pacifist. His cruise control engaged, and it told him to get between James and Laura.

# NOSTALGIA

Laura's beast mode interpreted Johnathan as attacker number two. What happened next was Biblical.

In the Old Testament there was a man named Jacob, the son of Isaac and grandson of Abraham. Jacob was making his way over to the land of Canaan to meet his bloodthirsty brother, Esau.

Then a mysterious figure appeared. Depending on the translation, this being was arguably an angel. Even more astounding, this being may have been God. It wrestled Jacob until dawn.

Jacob won but was given a permanent limp. Then he forced God, the angel, this creature, to bless him. From then on, Jacob was known as Israel.

The fight between Laura and Johnathan Jesus Christ did not last until dawn.

It lasted from 3:17:56 p.m. to 3:18:01 p.m.

A swift kick to the balls of God, with the reckoning force of a well-cared-for, steel-toed combat boot.

Laura's name was still Laura.

She wasn't looking for a blessing.

Three hours after the confrontation, Wendy and Laura partook in incredibly sinful behavior with each other. They were to develop what Dr. Simon Kant would have diagnosed as "pathological sexuality of the homosexual kind."

The rest of the evening was most definitely of this kind—homosexual, that is—and it was mind-boggling. Insane. Deviant. Glorious.

God destroyed Sodom and Gomorrah for such activities.

Wendy and Laura woke up the next morning to live another day, their bodies aching with sexual exhaustion.

# 14

## Rescue Operation

"Oh, that's the van," Ted said. "That's it. Right there."

It was real. Right in front of them.

"I don't see anyone in the driver's seat," Mike said, stepping out of their car.

Ted called after him, "What are you doing?"

Mike was already on his way toward the van. He turned around to shrug, before reaching the large sliding door.

Ted locked up. Grit his teeth. Chewed on his tongue.

Then Mike opened the door.

Mike perked up. "Sara?"

A woman was sitting against the wall opposite Mike, staring at the floor. Ted rushed over to see who it was.

"It's not her," Ted said.

"Fuck it. Let's at least get her out of here. Hey, uh..." Mike was trying to talk to the woman now. "We're here to get you out of this shit."

She didn't move.

"Have a name?" Mike asked.

She looked up at them.

"Sophia," she said. "So. So. Sophia. Some eyes. Olives."

"That's great stuff, Sophia," Mike said, reaching into the van. Sophia slapped him away, hesitated, and shuffled her way out of the van by herself.

Ted, feeling sweat breaking through his pores, pleaded, "Let's go. Let's go."

Sophia walked with them, as if she was an elderly woman being led across the street. To all appearances, she looked fine and fully capable. She was in her thirties, as tall as Mike, with short brown hair.

However, Sophia seemed unable to make decisions on her own. She let them help her into the car, eyes glazed, breathing steady. She gave no hint of fear or happiness. Her expression matched that of a person listening to the weather channel as a podcast: blank and bored.

Mike drove the car out of the lot.

"Well, that was easy," Mike said. "Kind of anticlimatic."

"Yeah. It was. Isn't it anticlimactic? Anticlimatic sounds like something out of *An Inconvenient Truth*."

"The truth is you can just shut up."

Ted looked at Sophia in the back seat. "Uh, do you have a family? Somewhere we can take you? I guess?"

"Olives. Like eyes. Olivia. Sophia," she said.

"I'm not sure I follow."

"Little olives."

Sophia didn't seem to be speaking to anyone in particular. She kept reaching for the door, stopping, placing her hands in her lap, and repeating the process.

"Where is Sara?" Ted asked.

Nothing.

Looking at Sophia through the rearview mirror, Mike said, "Let's take her to the police station. See if there's a missing person thing."

Neither Ted nor Mike had thought about next steps. They had planned to confront Mr. Satin, but that hadn't happened. They had planned for Sara to be there, but that hadn't happened.

· · • ● • ● • • ·

Mr. Satin dropped a brown bag full of thrifty clothing, and groceries from the shop nearby, at his feet.

"What is this?" he said.

Sara, standing next to him, blinked.

"She really left? After everything I said about what that will mean?" Mr. Satin's lips continued moving during the pause that followed. "Maybe I was too hard?"

Pause. Moving lips. Words without sound.

"Maybe I did more damage than I thought, so she just doesn't understand what I mean."

Dead air. Hand motions.

"You understand, right?" he asked Sara. He didn't wait for a response. He walked around to the driver's side. Sara stepped up into the passenger seat.

"No," Mr. Satin said, "sit in the back. You can't sit there. I left the door open for you to get in the back."

Sara opened the door, closed it, stepped into the back, closed the door.

"That's better. Sit right there. Nice view, right? Best we got."

He pulled out of the parking spot, crushing just-purchased organic eggs produced by cage-free chickens and blowing up a gallon of acidophilus milk as he drove over them. Thick yellow yolk crept over the pavement, swirling in bleach-white probiotic dairy liquid.

"I still have to do it," he said. He gave a sigh, adjusted the glasses to the bridge of his nose. "I have to do it for all the eyes to really see."

## 15

## SACRILEGE

"I thought we were picking up food?" James said. "I saw you can get a hot dog for only a dollar fifty."

He coughed. His throat was still trying to believe it had enough room to breathe normally.

"You can, and we will. We need something else, too," Johnathan Jesus Christ said.

They were strolling through the aisles, eating samples, dutifully throwing empty cups into open trash bins.

"You have a hard time letting go of the indiscretions of others, yes?" Johnathan said.

"You mean that woman knocking us down on our ass? To be honest, there was a lot of screaming going on in my head. I froze up."

"Sometimes the demons of action force us into inaction."

Johnathan Jesus Christ stopped. He was astounded by the magnificence of his own words.

"Sure," James said, "and how do your balls feel?"

They didn't feel well. Johnathan was able to walk normally, but it took plenty of hesitant limping to make it to Member$Mart.

"Ah! Here we are," Johnathan said, pointing down the aisle. "There! These are on instant rebate this week, it just so happens."

Motorcycle helmets, the kind with fully tinted glass windows, lined two pallets.

"Why do we need these?" James asked.

"Another trial. You trust me, right? I can trust you with my life if I needed to?"

"Completely," James said.

James had so far been unimpressed with the messiah. He was told to have restraint, let ball kickers be ball kickers, and resist the temptation of vengeance. The Old Testament seemed sexier, with all the shows of power.

"Good. I think of you as a brother. Did you know that James was the brother of Jesus? In the Bible?"

"No. I didn't know that."

"I had a brother once. He's dead now, though."

This caught James off guard. He hadn't heard a word of Johnathan's personal life, outside his divinity and his odd aphorisms.

Johnathan Jesus Christ did have a brother who died. What he wasn't mentioning was that his parents had both died on the same day. Johnathan's brother, Jacob, was eighteen at the time.

A video game called *One Winged Angel* was extremely popular at the time. Jacob played the game on his computer every evening, often in single player mode, but he was especially fond of playing multiplayer all-out battles online.

Jacob was a gamer who found it impossible to play without telling strangers they could suck his dick and get "raped by hobbits." This may sound rather profane to those who have not entered into the voice-capable world of online gaming.

It isn't. It is very much the norm.

One day, Jacob went into his bedroom to find that his gaming laptop was gone. Frantically, he ran around the house shouting. His parents told him they had hidden it because a letter had come in the mail saying Jacob wouldn't be able to graduate high school with his current grades.

"When will I get it back, then?" he said.

"When you graduate high school," his father said.

Johnathan had moved out of the house by this point but was planning on staying over the weekend. When he arrived, nobody answered the door.

He tried calling his dad. No answer.

He tried calling his mom. No answer.

He tried calling his brother. No answer.

In the days leading up to his arrival, he remembered his dad telling him a passcode to the garage. The garage door opened on his first attempt.

"Hello? Hey, anyone here?" he asked the silent home.

He found his parents in the living room. Both of them were bleeding from their heads onto the carpet. Johnathan started hyperventilating, stopped, then went into autopilot.

He checked his mom's pulse. Nothing.

He checked his dad's pulse. Something.

Johnathan couldn't remember the pin to his phone to call 911. Most modern phones don't require a pin for 911, but his brain couldn't remember this fact.

"Fuck! Fuck! Fuck!"

Once he unlocked the phone, the 911 operator talked him through his panic.

His father had been unconscious for four hours.

The Narrator knows how it all unfolded: Jacob had told his parents he had a surprise for them, but they had to first close their eyes and turn around. As they did, he took out his dad's 9mm handgun and fired at his mom's head. She dropped. His dad jolted, spun around, and was knocked unconscious by a bullet that grazed his temple.

Jacob had dug around in his parents' bedroom, found his gaming laptop, and tossed it in a backpack. He threw it over his shoulder and made off with his dad's crotch rocket.

Inexperienced with the motorbike, he took a turn far too sharply and without a helmet. He was dead within two hours of shooting his own parents.

Their father died before he made it to the hospital. This was how Johnathan Jesus Christ was reborn a messiah, a God that could save the human race by purchasing a helmet for the good of all living things.

"How did your brother die?" James asked.

"Act of God," Johnathan answered.

The two walked toward the food court, where three dollars' worth of USDA all-beef hot dogs awaited them. James always added onions and mustard. Johnathan preferred relish to onions.

"These are kosher, yes?" Johnathan asked.

"Yes," the cashier said.

"Only the blessed for the best," Johnathan said, flashing an open-mouthed smile to James.

"Sure," said the cashier. "That'll be three dollars and twenty cents."

"Excuse me?" Johnathan said.

James cut in. "That's just with tax."

"Oh."

Johnathan had three dollars in his hand, but he stopped short of handing them to the cashier.

"Sir, are you going to pay with that?"

Johnathan whispered, "Tax? In the house of God?"

"What?"

James could see a change creeping over Johnathan's face, the first time he had seen it happen in their short relationship.

Johnathan felt a mix of fear and intense energy flow outward from his spine, a match dropped into a puddle of gasoline. James watched him walk away from the cashier toward the condiments table.

"Uh, sir? Aren't you going to—"

"No more!" Johnathan shouted. "No more!"

He tried to flip the table over but failed. It was weighted down by mega-size condiment dispensers and pushed up against the wall.

James threw mustard packets at the cashier's face and started screaming. He ran over to the condiments table and helped his savior flip the table over, like a true disciple.

"No more taxing blessed meats! No more!" Johnathan shouted at the food court full of patrons.

James ran over to the nearest table, knocking cheeseburgers and soda cups off with divine howls.

"Dude, what the heck is this?!" a man said as his fries scattered on the floor.

James stared into his soul. "This is the house of God, motherfucker!"

"No more! No more!" Johnathan, in his religious fervor, was being dragged out by an LP (another acronym! Give more!)—Loss Prevention, security for retailers. James grabbed the two purchased helmets out of the cart and ran to catch up with Johnathan at the exit.

He turned back to the silent onlookers, seated throughout the cafeteria, shouting, "This is more like a house of criminals! Twenty cents? Are you serious?"

James had been attempting to quote the Bible. He failed.

Jesus had said: *"My house shall be called the house of prayer; but ye have made it a den of thieves."*

"This isn't a church, you maniac!" the now-fryless member said.

Remember: A penis, in some translations of the Bible, is called a member.

A Member$Mart member, in contemporary English, is *not* a penis. This is true even if said member has a penis.

The evolution of language is a beautiful thing.

# 16

## Canada Goose

Goose decided to meet a long-time friend in Manitoba, Canada, for a hunting trip. The goose incident at Member$Mart was something he could turn in his favor, allowing for a vacation of which he was in dire need. He didn't need to bring his own guns and, to cut on cost, he was able to take a cross-country bus at his leisure.

He napped with sunlight on his face, carried into a stress-free slumber. But then he woke up.

"Where is it?" a man said.

The man was sitting next to Goose, in what had been an empty seat before he fell away into dreams forgotten.

"Pardon?" Goose asked.

"What you owe, where is it?"

"I don't owe anything. I paid before I got on."

Goose realized that this man had nothing to do with the bus, or his paid fare. Not at all. The man was leaning in close, his clothes smelling of compost with high onion content. His breath stank of old cheese.

"You haven't paid," the man said.

"I think you have the wrong person."

"You'd like that, wouldn't you? But I see it. Nobody else does, but I see it."

"What?"

"I can see your aura," the man said, before speaking in what sounded like French. He had a Bluetooth headset hanging over his right ear. Seeing it, Goose felt relieved that it might be a bizarre misunderstanding.

"Are you talking to me or someone else? Sorry, I don't know French and I—"

"No, you know *all* languages."

A sense of sudden helplessness crept up from Goose's stomach, like realizing he had stepped into quicksand. He glanced around at the other passengers. Everybody else was disconnected from the present, jacked into their phones and tablets. Some were sleeping. The only one who looked concerned was a woman sitting directly behind him.

When Goose made eye contact with her, her eyes shifted quickly to the screen of her cell phone. Goose was unable to see this, but her phone was dead and all she was looking at was a black screen. She feigned false interest and tapped the screen.

The man kept sputtering out French. He was shaking.

"I need to use the bathroom," Goose said.

"No, you don't! Because you never eat." The man pulled out a large hunting knife. "And now you will never—"

Goose grabbed for the knife, screaming, "Help! He's got—he's got a knife!"

Some people woke up. They were now watching Goose struggling with the Frenchman, who didn't say a word. He was breathing heavily, with spit shooting out with each heave of resistance.

"He's trying to kill me!" Goose shouted.

The bus came to a stop. People watched in frozen agony as the knife slit open Goose's hand. The Frenchman half-stood over Goose, pushing the knife down into Goose's side.

And into his side.

And into his side.

And into his neck.

And into his side.

The Frenchman stopped, swung the bloody knife up, and started shouting at the passengers. He waved the knife around and pointed to the front of the bus.

Goose watched, gasping at the blood leaking out of his body, as the passengers stood up from their seats. They left the bus, one by one, in tears. In fear.

They were leaving him behind. Leaving him alone.

Then Goose passed out.

• • • ● • ● • • •

Mr. Satin had lived in Seattle for six years, into his early twenties. He would go on road trips to music festivals, where he met several people.

"How can you see?" his girlfriend at the time asked him.

"My sunglasses are specialized, prescription lens," he lied. "I can see better than you, I bet."

"Your eyes are crazy cool, like you're wearing those contact lenses that Marilyn Manson wears."

She died, blissfully, of an ecstasy overdose in the middle of a concert. Mr. Satin knelt down, holding her in his arms, with the eyes of strangers piercing him.

He felt nothing.

Then he felt everything.

He felt that he should die with her. That was when people dropped. Three people fell down, waking him from his self-degradation long enough to realize something beautiful was beginning.

"Whoa, you alright?"

"Did they just faint?"

People were crying.

*Did they faint?* he thought. *It doesn't matter.*

He felt in his pockets, looking for something to take him away. Something to provide an overdosed path to the afterlife. Then more people fell. And more.

He chose to live. Something had become of him. Emotional, internal self-mutilation was tearing others down. A metaphysical knockout punch.

He later tried it in supermarkets. At intersections.

One by one, people would collapse.

Cars would collide.

It wasn't delusion. It was real.

His last week in Seattle, while with some friends at a house party, he heard gunfire outside. A man, wanting to kill everything around him, walked in shooting. Nirvana blared through speakers on the front porch.

Mr. Satin waited upstairs in a locked bathroom, with a trembling girl.

"Hey, just keep your eyes on me. Everything will be okay," he said. "What's your name?"

"Jackie."

People screamed downstairs.

One person ran upstairs, yelling, "He's gonna kill me!"

There was a pounding on the bathroom door.

Another gun shot. No more pounding.

Mr. Satin swung the door open, and his self-loathing filled the hallway. The armed man slumped to the floor.

"Holy shit, holy shit, holy—" Jackie was shaking.

"Just keep your eyes on me," Mr. Satin said. "Everything will be fine."

He walked over to the shooter, pulled a handgun out of the man's side holster.

"What are you doing?" she asked.

Mr. Satin dragged the shooter over to the wall near the stairwell and leaned him up against it. The shooter's head was freshly shaved, and his face was covered in green paint. His eyes were closed, breathing easy.

"I'm standing up to a shooter," Mr. Satin said. "Trying to save lives."

A tear dripped down her face, and she asked, "How are you doing this?"

"Well, he killed this girl who was hiding with me in the bathroom. Right before I fought him off and shot him in the head. I just met the girl, too," he said. "I think her name was Jackie."

You can ride a low-cost tour bus in Seattle where a man shouts jokes through a megaphone and shows you the house where Kurt Cobain's body was found. They drive through Seattle every week and talk about the First Hill massacre of 2007 in which the only survivor single-handedly stopped a mass murderer. The hero had been found writhing on the floor, suffering from a blackout migraine.

# 17

## Deux Ex Machina

Mike was walking across the parking lot, high off a new world of meaning. He and Ted had saved the life of a woman being used by a monster of a man. There were more to save. This really was it.

He walked toward Member$Mart in a zigzag motion, in order to avoid goose droppings. A new employee, a very shy woman, worked at the gas station since Goose was gone. She would try to move the geese away by saying, "Oh dear. Oh dear. Shoo! Go away! Oh dear."

She was just loud enough for Mike to hear. Normally, everyone in the parking lot could hear Goose clear as day, when he would shout. His replacement was speaking quiet gibberish in comparison. Returning customers were confused, thinking something may be wrong, when they walked from their cars into the store. They didn't know why. They only knew something was amiss, as if someone had turned off all the white noise from Goose's shouting with the flip of a switch.

There were no more *godflabbits, get-the-heck-away-dang-its, what-you-wanna-fights*, or even *what-do-ya-think-you're-doings*. It was eerie. The geese had defeated their greatest enemy. They had done so via martyrdom.

Mike saw a car drive straight into a line of shopping carts. Depending on where a store is throughout the world, a cart may be called a shopping trolley or basket.

Mike was about to spring into action but noticed two people slumped over between two parked cars just a few yards from him. He went to them instead.

"Hey, you alright?" he said, leaning down and setting his hand on a shoulder.

There was no response. Both of them lay limp, still breathing but unresponsive. Mike could no longer hear the woman at the gas station. He heard someone stepping up behind him.

"Hello, Michael."

· · · ● · ● · ● ● · ·

Ted was inside Member$Mart. He was buying a hot dog and soda combo for less than two dollars. A fine deal.

Wheeling himself up to a table, and after covering the mystery meat with a heaped pile of mustard and onions, he was ready to eat. Mike was often late, so Ted was taking advantage of the situation. Unfortunately, a person collapsed into him and knocked his meal to the floor.

"Hey!" Ted said, conveying his desperation, anger, and blame in a single word.

Then he noticed it wasn't just this one fellow who had face-planted. It seemed that everyone in the entire store had done so. Collectively, they made a noise like plastic rustling in a cold winter breeze: *duff, fudda fudda fudda*. People fell everywhere in a brief, human rainfall.

Ted thought he was having a nightmare.

At this point, he spotted Mike walking through the front entrance. It was easy to spot him, the sole person trudging in the sea of fallen shoppers.

Mike looked around. It was easy to spot Ted, sitting upright at a table in a football helmet.

"Mike! What the hell is going on?" Ted shouted over at him.

"He's here," Mike said, making his way to Ted.

Ted didn't need to ask who he was. He already knew, and he could see Mr. Satin walking through the entrance with a woman a few steps behind.

Mike looked ghastly. Without a word, he sat to Ted's right.

Mr. Satin was taking his time. Every one of the unconscious people seemed to annoy him. He stomped on their hands, legs, or arms. Two tables away from Ted, he stopped and kicked the face of a mother with his boot. Her child sat asleep in her cart. This was when Ted noticed Mr. Satin was specific about whom he targeted in his annoyance.

They were all women.

Finally, Mr. Satin made it over to the table where Ted and Mike sat. Sweat dripped down Mike's face.

"Everyone has a plan," Mr. Satin said. He threw a right hook at Mike's jaw. Mike spat out some blood, slipped out of consciousness, and Mr. Satin continued. "Until they get punched in the mouth."

Ted, frozen but feeling oddly safe in his football helmet, couldn't think of anything to say.

"I could feel his muscle tissues collapse under my force," Mr. Satin said, watching himself shift his face toward the ceiling. "It's ludicrous these mortals even attempt to enter my realm."

He shook his head, adjusting his round, blue spectacles. "I just want to conquer people and their souls. I'm a dreamer. I have to dream and reach for the stars." He lifted his arm, swiping at the dust. "And if I miss a star? Then I grab a handful of clouds."

What Ted didn't realize was that Mr. Satin had been memorizing these lines over the past four days. He listened to audio readings of Mike Tyson quotes on repeat. Finding that these were the most intimidating, and—not really knowing how to talk properly to other people socially—he repeated them daily. This was an amazing performance and had an effect that was even stronger than he was expecting.

"So, Ted, where do we go from here? The way I see it, there is one of two paths to take. One way is to let your good, bleeding friend here get a low-boh."

"A low-boh?"

"Yeah, a lobotomy. You know exactly what the hell I mean by that, right? Don't act like you don't. You took one of my eyes last week. I had to bring a spare along today." Mr. Satin pointed behind him with his thumb. The woman, standing about ten feet behind him, stared silently.

It wasn't Sara.

"Oh, her?" Mr. Satin went on. "That's Ashley. Why don't you join us, Ted, if you're worried about her?"

"The second path?" Ted asked.

"Yes. You come with me and get a low-boh of your own. You're a rare find. I see color through your eyes. I can't just smack an ice pick to your face and hope I do it right. I need to restrain you. I need to be really careful. You're like some fragile china that's just sitting there and never being used. I can't risk losing you because you'll just end up passing out and stabbing yourself in your kitchen."

"That has happened, actually. I'll live."

"I'm glad. I'd help you if you go with me. The guy who came up with the transorbital low-boh may have even prescribed some frontal lobe damage as a potential cure to your problems, if he was still around. It's either you or this idiot here." Mr. Satin was referring to Mike, who was drooling blood all over his shirt.

The inventor of the transorbital lobotomy would likely have rubber-stamped Ted for a good ol' face puncture. Dr. Freeman was reliable for decisions like that.

"Why are you doing this?" Ted said.

"You don't know? I had to read the Torah as a kid. I had to read the Tanakh. It helped me become a man. The truth is, what's happening is direction from God. As everybody knows, He had a very important rule that I'll never forget," Mr. Satin said, struggling to hold back his anger. "An eye for an eye."

"What if," he said from the driver's seat, "you could cut out mental illness like a tumor?"

"It doesn't sound like anyone could really do that," Ted said.

"It doesn't matter if you can, Teddy. What matters is your ability to sell the results either way. Walter Jackson Freeman II was one of the greatest salesmen of all time, lobotomizing war vets and misbehaving children. Doing this to an adult, he was quoted as calling the brain damage surgically induced childhood! Can you believe that? The VA brought him on as a consultant. Over two thousand people received a low-boh following his methods, of the same ice-pick variety that I've adopted. He's a mentor of mine, really, only separated from me by time."

# NOSTALGIA

Mr. Satin was right. A neurologist really did this. The VA had marveled at the change in a patient's behavior after brain damage: They were easier to manage. Dr. Freeman even made house calls for delinquent children in his mobile van. He had invented the ice-pick lobotomy but never won an award for his more "humane" and "less invasive" version of a lobotomy.

A rumor developed that people were calling his van the *lobotomobile*.

An ice pick to the face required only some electroshock to knock the patient unconscious first. The frontal lobe damage was meant to make them right as rain.

An older type of the procedure, in which neurosurgeons would saw into the top of the head, involved placing a rod lined with a special cutting wire into the top of the head. Significant lacerations would be made to the brain tissue via the sharp wire. The special rod was called a *leucotome*, and this method was called a *leucotomy*. The inventor, a Dr. Egas Moniz, won a Nobel Prize in 1949 for his efforts.

Freeman took pride in his work. He had performed surgery on almost twenty children. One of his patients died when he paused to pose for a photo during surgery, killing the man by penetrating too far into the brain.

The picture didn't turn out that well.

Ain't life grand?

"Though," Mr. Satin added, "brain damage doesn't result in a completely docile individual. It's really just an extreme tool that assists with the added threat of repercussions. If they try to leave, try to kill themselves, or any similar nonsense? I go North Korean on them. I'll kill their family, their lover, their friends. All of them have social media profiles where they literally list people as family members. This makes my life much easier."

"You're fucked up," Ted said.

"Hey now! I've only had to follow through on those kinds of threats *two* times. One time, three years ago, a girl went and slit her wrists in the bathtub. I had to kill her niece just so the others would know I'm very serious about these things. I felt miserable about that. You know what? I had to make a point *again,* yesterday, for that poor girl you kidnapped from my van. How do you feel about that?"

Ted's heart dropped into his stomach.

"What did you do?" he said.

"What did *I* do? No, don't blame me for what *you* did. I took into account the fact that she didn't do this on her own. You influenced her, likely taking her without much input from her. I only killed her younger brother because of all that. She's back at my place, you know, safe and sound after applying an ice pick for the second time. Maybe you'll get to say hi before she helps me tie you to the kitchen table."

At times, Dr. Freeman had performed transorbital lobotomies more than once on the same patient. The reason he finally had his license revoked was for killing a woman, due to giving her a third lobotomy. About 15 percent of his patients died of brain hemorrhaging, as she did.

It has been recorded that his procedure cost around $200. His license was revoked after performing $600 worth of procedures on the same woman. Using inflation, his services may have cost a patient almost $6,000 in 2016 America.

Mr. Satin had taken note of these things, viewing Freeman as an entrepreneurial hero who took his show on the road.

A sedan came flying past on Mr. Satin's left-hand side. The driver of that car was wearing a motorcycle helmet, and it looked like the passenger was attempting to put an even larger helmet on himself.

"The fuck is this?" Mr. Satin said under his breath, watching through Ashley's eyes.

• • • ● • ● • • •

James, speeding up, was concerned. Not because it was raining, and not because the car had little tread.

"There's no other car out here," he said to Johnathan Jesus Christ. "Why do you need to jump out in front of one?"

"It's man versus machine, James," Johnathan shouted, for James to hear him clearly.

"You sure you want this?" James shouted back. "And why are we wearing helmets, anyways?"

"Not just me that wants this. God said so, and I agree. Says so right on the back of my card, James. As for the helmet?" Johnathan stuffed his head into his full-face motorcycle helmet. James couldn't see it, but Johnathan flashed a smile through the dark black window. James couldn't hear it, but Jesus said in a muffled voice, "Safety first!"

Johnathan Jesus Christ proceeded to barrel-roll out of the passenger side door faster than a starving child could say grace.

# 18

## This Way and That Way

There was no way the van was going to avoid the body of a god flying around on the highway. A chaotic combination. An overcorrection. The right front tire shattering into the helmet of Johnathan Jesus Christ had shifted the side of the vehicle upward.

Ashley sat blankly, restrained by her passenger-side seatbelt.

Mr. Satin cracked his glasses against the steering wheel and reeled back in his seat.

Ted, flung into the air, was traveling back in time.

He was in the ocean, not far from a San Diego beach in 2006, having failed to ride a wave with a bodyboard. The wave fell upon him, pulling him under with a spin that made his body spiral out of control. He was beaten this way and that by invisible, violent forces. Coming to the surface in time to catch his breath, his board had floated up and bopped him in the face.

In 2016, Ted was ejected from the vehicle to the pavement, with only scrapes and bruises. He was, otherwise, remarkably unharmed. His neck hurt but luckily didn't break. Canada geese had nothing on this man.

He was alive. His helmet had saved his life.

Dazed, he lifted himself off the ground. The van had landed right-side up, with glass blown out of every window. The windshield was split all to hell, impossible to see through. Ashley sat unconscious in the passenger seat, quietly dying due to internal bleeding.

Mr. Satin was standing next to the van. He was furious. There was a gun somewhere on the road, flung from the van just like Ted's body. Even though his glasses were cracked, Mr. Satin kept them on. On or off, they had no impact on the quality of his perception.

Ted spotted a crowbar nearby. He picked it up. It was cold, wet, covered with sand and grit.

"I can't believe," Ted said, "that this is my fucking life right now."

· · · ● · ● · · ·

James kept driving. He had seen the crucifixion of his reality through the rearview mirror, resulting in the death of his savior. Voices echoed around him in crowded shouting, a mixture of unrecognizable babble, bursting about him. He couldn't see straight. He pulled over and sobbed loudly into his palms.

· · · ● · ● · · ·

Mr. Satin and Ted found themselves almost incapable of fighting. Ted kept traveling, leaving Mr. Satin blind on the highway as Ted's consciousness stumbled in the past.

Ted was surprised to find he no longer collapsed during his travels but was partially aware of his surroundings in the present—much like when he was hospitalized.

Mr. Satin's blindness came with a terrible ringing in the ears. He stumbled around, losing his bearings, as Ted froze in place. Ted was able to take a partial swing with his crowbar before he found himself playing tee-ball as a small child.

If one adds the letter "d" to the end of "crowbar," it results in a crowbar that can tell stories... or is it a crow that can tell tales?

The world may never know.

Ted's childhood shenanigans with small aluminum bats resulted in the crowbar flying out of his hands. It flew over Mr. Satin's shoulder and into the back seat of the van.

Mr. Satin knocked Ted to the ground, sending Ted reeling back to his teenage years, and Mr. Satin rolled on the ground in agony.

Ted relived losing his virginity, when he had unprotected sex with a girl who pushed him off her after orgasming forty seconds in. Before then, he thought "blue balls" were a myth.

He was wrong.

Forty is a factor of four. This reminded Ted of Viagra sales.

This reminds The Narrator of dangers in the four-hour chub.

• • • ● • ● • • •

James adjusted the car mirror, looking at himself. His eyes were bloodshot. He wiped the snot from his face with his sleeve.

"You're fine. We're fine," he said. "We're good. We're great. Shit happens. People die. Everybody knows Jesus died. Jesus! He just died! Fuck!"

Expletives fell out of his mouth like teeth might in Dr. Simon Kant's dreams. The demons that James had weren't in his dreams, they were in his waking life. The everyday.

"I'm fine," he heard a voice say. "I'm okay, James."

"Johnathan?"

"Jesus Christ."

A smile spread across James's face. He was laughing through tears.

Some people believe that if you dream of your teeth falling out, it's due to feeling guilt over something you said in your waking life. Dr. Simon Kant felt grief over James meeting Johnathan Jesus Christ.

James experienced no guilt. He felt salvation.

• • • ● • ● • • •

Mr. Satin gained his bearings, but only because someone in the distance was taking a look at him in an approaching vehicle.

James. Squinting. Approaching hesitantly. Mr. Satin could see Ted standing up, close to the wrecked van, helmet on, frozen in time. Lost in time.

Then Ted was back.

Ted looked at the driver.

"Help!" Ted said, before being knocked down by Mr. Satin.

"Fuck you, Ted! You had the option! You had the opportunity!" Mr. Satin said, lifting his foot and stomping down again.

James stepped out of the car. "Whoa! Everybody calm down!"

Ted stopped moving.

"You around, Ted?" Mr. Satin asked.

No response.

"Okay then."

Mr. Satin took a few steps back, trying to catch his breath.

Ted wasn't traveling. He snapped upward and made a run for the gun.

"No you don't!" Mr. Satin shouted, giving chase.

James did nothing. He was standing against the open driver's-side door. His mouth opened slightly, a look of disbelief on his face.

Ted was nearly on the gun when he cataplexed. His entire body gave out, and his limp body rolled forward with his momentum. Mr. Satin laughed, picked up the gun, and pointed it at James.

"Was that dead fucker your friend? The one who decided to kiss the fender of my van?"

"Yes," James said.

"Well, he really fucked everything up."

James didn't respond.

"This is my friend Ted," Mr. Satin said. "Seems he tripped and fell out of my van."

"Why is he wearing a football helmet?" James asked.

"Why the fuck was your friend wearing a motorcycle helmet?"

It dawned on James that events were connected in ways that he would never be able to comprehend.

"It's beyond us," James said. "One can't really know God."

"What?"

James could hear Johnathan Jesus Christ say, "Go with him."

"Why should I go with him?" James asked, aloud.

"With who?" Mr. Satin said. "Ted?"

But Ted was gone. James and Mr. Satin witnessed a miracle: Something became nothing.

## Frankie's Steakhouse: 1 / 5 stars

*Normally, the word "steakhouse" brings to mind five stars because I love me some steak. Eating meat. Bringing on the mashed potatoes and gravy. Passing out before I make it to my car in the parking lot.*

*Not here.*

*The bathroom floor was sticky. Not just under the urinals. The entire surface of the bathroom had evolved into some sort of glue-made-from-recycled-waste substance. I was a fucking spider trapped on a tape roll.*

*A small child cried for help from a bathroom stall, permanently fused to the shitter.*

*I barely made it out with my life, let alone with any leftover meat.*

*Each table had A1 sauce, and the waiter was well versed in wine pairing.*

— Reviewed by *MikeMan*

# 19

## HERE AND THERE

"You're saying," Mr. Satin said to James, "that he was Jesus?"

James was driving them to Mr. Satin's address, which was tapped into the GPS.

"Yes," James said.

"The guy who ate pavement and took a bite from my van?"

"Yeah," James said.

"And now he's telling you to help me out?"

"Yeah," James said.

"And you're okay just leaving his dead body, the girl's dead body, and my van all fucked up at the scene of an accident?"

"God," James quietly stated, with a pause entailing a drawn-out inhale, "is great."

"You're Muslim?"

James twisted his face, appalled. "No, they don't believe in Jesus."

"They do," Mr. Satin said, smugly.

"They do?"

"Not like you do, you know, with Jesus jumping in front of cars on the fucking highway. But yeah, they do."

James had pledged himself to Mr. Satin. He had seen him battle a man who snapped out of existence before his very eyes.

Mr. Satin went on. "But don't think about it. All I need help with, and I'm glad I'm getting it, is someone to babysit my ex-wife's kid."

He had no ex-wife. He did, though, have a boy at his apartment.

"His mother, Sophia, is at my place. We're trying to have a calm conversation. Be civil. But you know how women get, right?"

James coughed and tried not to think of Laura's fist having crashed into his windpipe.

"Yes," James said, "I do."

· · · ● · ● · · ·

Ted was gone.

Somewhere. Elsewhere.

Sometime. Elsewhen.

Further exposition. Even more. Lots.

Vague meandering.

Even The Narrator is at a loss for words.

Eofiapjf sdkfjpein wqpihjewofnvcmpo, fdlksdjfqpe dsf.

· · · ● · ● · · ·

Member$Mart had shut down to investigate why people fell over at the store. Every emergency service had arrived: police, ambulances, firefighters.

No lightning had struck the premises.

There wasn't a carbon monoxide leak.

People were beginning to think there was a terrorist attack.

Footage of the warehouse and the parking lot were being reviewed.

When all the customers had woken up confused, Mike knew exactly what had happened. The situation was crystal clear. He didn't stick around. He ran.

In his brain an acronym flashed like a neon sign: *GTFO*.

The acronym has as many syllables as the definition. One would be wise not to fool oneself into thinking that it is a verbal shorthand.

Ted was gone.

Mike made it to his car. A body was in his back seat.

"Ted?"

Ted sat up. "You were right. I have superpowers or some **shit**."

"You're bleeding."

"And I'm hungry."

"Okay, but you're still bleeding."

"Mike, if I focus, I think I can really do things. We need to act fast. We helped Sophia get out of Mr. Satin's van, but now he's reacting."

"I know. He punched me in the face, Ted."

"Oh, right."

"Yes, right," Mike said, moving his hand over his own chin.

"I have an idea, Mike. Let's go to BoJak's. This could be our last meal."

# 20

## Bullet Proof

In medieval times, heavy-ass armor was worn in battle.

Stephanie L. Kwolek invented Kevlar in 1965.

The United States Army signed a contract in 2016 with Kraig Biocraft Laboratories in hopes of developing *Dragon Silk*—genetically modified spider silk—body armor.

Bulletproof 360 was founded in 2013. They are associated with Bulletproof Coffee. If you shot someone after they enjoyed this coffee, the drink would have provided no known defense against gunpowder-propelled metal objects.

In 2016, Shannon—whom Ted met at a Biohackers group, and lover of Bulletproof Coffee—was on a road trip to inject blood into her vagina.

In 2017, cadet Hayley Weir collaborated with professor Ryan Burke to whip up some bullet-stopping goop. It could potentially reduce the amount of fabric worn by soldiers by 75 percent.

Mr. Purdy, in 1989, scrawled words of intolerance onto his own Kevlar armor before gunning down children.

Megan, Mike, and Ted all shared an inability to cook food without a microwave. As adult children, they waited for the waitress to make meals for them.

They sat in silence. Mike had a purple splotch gracing the side of his face. Attempts at controlled traveling hadn't achieved his hoped-for results.

The waitress dropped off the tacos, and a bearded man stumbled over from the bar to their table.

"Uh, what's up?" Mike asked.

"I hear, um, hear," the man slurred, "th-that there is a war hero over here."

Ted felt sweat come out of his pores. Megan raised an eyebrow.

"Damn right there is. This guy right here—back from Afghanistan with a bronze star and a Purple Heart," Mike said.

The man looked Ted over and noticed the football helmet on the table.

"Huh," he said. "Didn't you fall over when you came in here?"

"Yeah, that's me. I'm not a war hero, though. I didn't do anything," Ted said.

"That's what a real hero says," the man responded.

Mike chimed in. "He has brain trauma from an IED. He conks out sometimes when he's having flashbacks. We got him a Viking's helmet. Can you believe that none of the players would sign his helmet?"

"You gotta be shittin' me," the bearded drunk said under his breath. "Well, hell with it. This whole table, all of it, goes on my tab! Hear that? This guy went to war for us! Better than most them liberals that run for office. You know, there was a man ran for president who had a Bronze Star and a Purple Heart. Didn't win! Didn't win!"

"Thank you for your support," Mike said with cheer. "We need to go, so don't mind us as we finish our conversation in private."

The man stared at nobody in particular, saying, "I suppose." He made his way back to his barstool, repeating, "Didn't win! You believe that?"

Ted glared. "Dang it, Mike, I hate you sometimes. Let's get the heck out of here."

As the three stood up and walked to the exit, Mike Turnkey turned around to take a look at the bearded man.

"What's up, Mike?" Megan said.

Mike said, with a strong look of focus, "I could have sworn I recognized that guy from somewhere."

"We don't have time to talk to people, and now he thinks I'm a war veteran because you're a dick," Ted said.

"Right."

After they left, the faint sound of an audio recording came across the bar.

*"The internet is a great way to get on the net."*

It was Bob Dole's voice coming out of a treasured, misfit prototype.

"Right again!" shouted Travis Turnkey after reaching his seat. "And this guy couldn't make it to the pornographic Oval Office. Didn't win!"

Ted was traveling again.

"Okay, this might be working," Ted said.

"This is like remote viewing," Megan said. "You know the whole Stargate program? There was another one where they tried killing goats—"

Mike interrupted. "Stargate was a show."

"And a government program," Megan said, with no emotion.

"Guys, stop!" Ted said.

"Right," Mike said. "Ted, what do you see there?"

"Mr. Satin and Sara are just getting up from their table."

"Are they in a house? Apartment?"

"It's a bit crowded. There's a bar. I'm in a restaurant. The walls have weird art: animal people."

"What types of animals?"

"Uh, squid? And octopus. Not like Lovecraft crazy-type art. Not cutesy stuff like manga. Just... squid and octopus people. Wait, they stepped outside and are walking over to a door. Holy shit."

"What?"

"It's their apartment complex. I'm pretty sure, I think."

"Okay, we can work with that. Restaurant with bar, in same building as apartment complex."

"Yeah, same building."

Ted was back, saying, "I couldn't hold it. I didn't see anything else."

A flash struck across Mike's face. "I've been there."

"I know you have," Megan said. She was already typing away on her laptop.

"How? Were you with me?" Mike asked.

"No. This is why."

She spun the laptop around. The screen showed an authentic, high-quality restaurant review about a bathroom at a place called *Noose*.

### Noose Bar and Grill: 3 / 5 stars

*Donkey people artwork stared disapprovingly at me from above the urinals, accompanied by an overpowering smell of vanilla. Contrary to popular belief, a urinal cake is not a cake at all. Do not believe the lies.*

*I wished for a noose to hang myself in the stall with the broken lock. It never came. The guy in the stall next door was trying to come, though. He was vigorously jerking off so loud that he must have just discovered he had a dick. I don't know if he was successful.*

*The happy hour chicken wings were alright.*

— Reviewed by *MikeMan*

"Donkey people. I'm a hero," Mike said. "They had octopus and squid ones in the main dining area, too."

"We're going to Noose," Megan said. "Now let's fuck this guy with a two-foot warehouse dildo."

"We have almost everything," Mike said, "and I know we don't have enough time to grab a gun ourselves."

"Really?" Ted said. "Is that your excuse? Is that why you're going to bring a sword?"

Everything was on the coffee table: Ted's football helmet, Mike's sword, a kitchen knife, and black hooded masks.

"Shut up. The main problem is that Mr. Satin does have a gun. You can see the future sometimes, but neither of us can dodge bullets."

Megan jumped out of her seat.

"Wait, you need a bulletproof vest?"

"Yes."

"I can do even better."

"What do you mean?"

"It's already purchased. I'm even wearing it. Right now."

"Seriously?"

Indeed, she was wearing a vest.

Megan had purchased a massive amount of bitcoin when it was worth twenty-five dollars. Originally, she had not imagined it as some form of investment. She bought it because she wanted to get things off of Silk Road and, later, AlphaBay.

When her grandfather died, he chose to leave all his money to his favorite grandchild. This happened to be his only granddaughter: Megan Bukowski. At this point, she was already living off money she had made from selling an entirely different type of currency.

Imaginary in-game gold, which can only be found in video games, has its own worth online. Using two different automated applications, called "bots" to annoyed players, Megan "mined" resources within the games while she spent her time reading blog articles. Viewing memes. Watching cat videos. The resources she mined in the two games, across multiple web browsers and PC systems, paid her bills.

One of the games was *F&M4: Russian Hammer*, in which she recently won an achievement badge for killing the main character's parents in-game with an RPG (an acronym! It means rocket-propelled grenade!).

All $120,046 of her inheritance was dumped into bitcoin and the stock market, split equally. By 2016, Megan's bitcoin had become worth nearly a million dollars. Anything she wanted, she could buy.

She had not foreseen the future necessity of a bulletproof vest for the purpose of defending against live ammo. Instead, Megan had perceived a special item she found online as having mythical properties. The cost was just a number.

"In nineteen eighty-nine," she said, "there was this school shooting."

Megan told the story of Mr. Purdy, his anger against the "yellow bastards," and how he killed himself. She knew one other special piece of information that many people didn't.

"So, the crazy motherfucker who killed himself? He was wearing a bulletproof vest! The very one I'm wearing," she said.

"Um," Ted said, "why do we care that this vest was owned by a mass murderer?"

"Because of this!" Megan said, then attempted to dramatically rip open her buttoned shirt. She only succeeded in breaking off two of the top buttons. After a struggle, she gave up and slowly unbuttoned the rest of the buttons.

Over her heart was a message that Mr. Purdy had scrawled himself.

Ted looked on in awe. "You can't be serious?"

"Oh my fucking God," Mike said.

Smiling, Megan said, "Luckily for us, that racist dumbass couldn't spell worth shit."

The night before the shooting, Mr. Purdy had spent thirty minutes engraving the message of a religiously inclined and illiterate fanatic.

## DEATH TO THE GREAT SATIN

# 21

## INVASION

"Ladies," Mr. Satin said in his living room, addressing six stoic women, "today, I have the unfortunate chore of snuffing out a life. I don't take pleasure in this, believe me. I've only ever hurt each of you to make your lives less full of anxiety and emotion. This is something else. Now, Sophia?"

Sophia walked into the living room from the kitchen.

"Yes, Sophia. I understand that what happened to you was a bit outside of your control. Some people tore you away from me, but I don't share. I don't forgive actions of running away, either. Either way, I forgive you. How's that feel?"

Sophia said nothing.

"Right. Now," Mr. Satin said, looking to the others in the room, "Sophia's son is upstairs. In the nice, rooftop community room looking out across the—"

"Little olive," Sophia said.

"Sorry, was I talking to you?"

"Olive."

"What the fuck? Am I being too nice here? Is that what's happening?"

Loud whistling came from the kitchen.

"The tea!" Mr. Satin yelled, running into the kitchen. He fell down before he reached the stove. The steam whistle amplified his crushing migraine, pinning him to the floor.

"Get the fuck in here!" he shouted out.

All the women shuffled their way in. Each step toward Mr. Satin sent the shudder of an earthquake, from his temples, across his body. Beads of sweat dripped from his pores as he felt seasick and lost in the ocean of his kitchen floor.

He could see again.

"Someone get the goddamn tea!"

Water started frothing through the top of the kettle, dissipating in bubbles across the electric stove. Sophia lifted the kettle up and placed it to the side. Her other hand flicked the heat off.

Mr. Satin, with considerable effort, picked himself up from the floor.

"You're the only one who can pick that shit up and turn the heat off. An award in the special Olympics of my fucking life."

He picked up the kettle, walked to the dining table, and poured it into a mug with a teabag. Across from him was a stack of plastic cups. As his tea steeped, he filled up cups with tap water.

"Okay, now, everybody gets water. Fuck." Mr. Satin sighed, the last of his motion sickness leaving him. "You know, I was going to have Sophia open her mouth so I could pour boiling water down her stupid throat. But, you know what? I'm feeling thankful. I've been on the edge of death almost daily. Yet you all come to my aid whenever the black hole in my head is pulling me in." He lifted his arms up and down like a puppet. "Help! I've fallen and I can't get up! And there you all come, with no exception. All of you come.

"What do you call that, if not love? You could all step out together. Leave me to writhe and die. An infant. Incapable of taking care of himself."

He shifted himself to face Sophia. "I love you, Sophia. I do. Again, I forgive you. So, because I don't want you to see anything upstairs, I'll only take Sara with me. Hear that? You don't have to see it. That's because I love you."

"Little olive."

"Sure, little olive. Like a little eye, right? Funny thing. An olive can look just like a little eye. You're making me hungry. I've never eaten someone's eyes before."

"Little olive."

"Sophia, I'm not going to eat his fucking eyes, okay? Let's go, Sara. Be right back, everybody."

• • • ● • ● • • •

Ted sat with his back up against the wall of the stairwell.

"Teddy," Sara said, "we're leaving. We're going to the elevator in a moment."

"Okay. What floor are you on?"

"I don't know."

"How do you not—" Ted began, then caught himself in the shameful act of dismissing brain damage. "Uh, I got an idea. I'll just look through the little stairwell window on each floor until I see you."

"But Satin will know you are looking at us."

"He doesn't know who is looking, right? Just that someone is looking?"

"I don't know for sure. I think so."
"Great. We'll be fine."

Mr. Satin and Sara stepped out of the apartment.

"Please keep your eyes on me."

He leaned forward, pressed the key into the deadbolt, and swung the lock into place.

"On the first try. Nice."

They walked to the elevator, hit the button, and waited.

A man stepped out of a nearby apartment, locked his door, and went for the elevator.

"How's it going?" the man said, pushing the down button.

"Life is good," Mr. Satin said, smiling.

The doors of one elevator opened. Two people were inside.

"We're going down," they said.

"That's me!" the man said, stepping in.

As the door was closing, the three of them fell to the floor.

Mr. Satin shook his head and said, "We were here first."

The second elevator opened, going up.

"That's us."

Mr. Satin and Sara stepped in. The doors closed.

"Huh," Mr. Satin said, "I just caught some asshole staring at me from the stairwell. He was just standing there, peeking in."

Ted stepped out into the hallway.

"What apartment is it?"

Nothing.

"Sara?"

Nothing.

A door opened. A woman stepped into the hallway.

"Sophia?"

Sophia looked over.

"Olive," she said.

He ran over and entered the apartment. "Everyone, let's go. Come on, come on."

Nobody moved.

Ted anxiously pleaded. "Please. We don't have, like, time and shit!"

He started pushing everyone toward the door.

"Tell them I told you," Sara said. She was standing next to him.

"Listen up. I'm working with Sara."

Heads turned. All eyes focused.

"And—" Ted tilted his head slightly. "What? Ah, okay. So, I'm going to keep Mr. Satin in a black hole. Forever. I know what he has done to you, and—and your families are okay. They are waiting for you."

• • • ● • ● • • •

Megan was sitting in the lobby. Her legs moved restlessly.

"Come on, come on," she said under her breath.

Her phone vibrated. She looked at it.

"Finally."

The elevator doors opened.

"Hey!" she said, "I'm with Sara."

• • • ● • ● • • •

"Yo," Ted said, stepping into the stairwell. "You ready?"

"Motherfucker, even gotta ask that?" Mike said. He drew his sword.

"Okay. We need to go to the top floor. The kid's up there. There's some guy watching him, who is working with Mr. Satin somehow. Be careful."

"Fuck him. Let's do it."

Ted knelt down, put on his helmet. Then fell over.

"Ted! Piece of shit, get up!"

Ted didn't move.

"Fuck fuck fuck."

Mike took a step toward the stairs, took a step toward Ted, took a step back toward the stairs, and then started making his way up.

• • • ● • ● • • •

James sat on a large leather sofa with his back toward the community room door, watching a boy playing with Lego people. The boy kept picking them up, smashing them together, and dropping them to the floor.

"Pretty intense fight there," James said.

"Yeah." the boy said.

Mr. Satin walked in, asking, "How's our boy doing?"

James looked back over his shoulder. "He's doing fine. His Lego men aren't."

"Sara," Mr. Satin said, "I need to take a piss. Walk with me."

"Seriously? You can't even go to the bathroom without her?"

Mr. Satin walked to the bathroom with Sara.

"You just ignoring me?" James said.

"James," Johnathan Jesus Christ's voice said, "let him go. This is his cross to bear. Do you mock a blind man for his cane?"

· · · ● · ● · ● · · ·

James said, quietly so that his God could barely hear, "A little fucked up to compare a woman to a cane."

Mike looked into the community room. A man was sitting, facing away from Mike, watching a child playing on the floor. Mike opened the door as slowly and as quietly as he could. As he entered, one foot placed carefully before the other, he raised the sword.

The child looked up.

James laughed, then asked, "What's up, little man? Somethin' off?"

Mike blacked out.

· · · ● · ● · ● · · ·

"Kid, have a problem? The fight over? Who won?" James asked.

Evan, Sophia's child, watched Mike lock up. Mike's face distorted, reddened with bulging eyes and teeth clenched.

James looked up at the window behind Evan, catching the reflection of a man swinging a sword.

Johnathan, the messiah who had recently died in a leap of faith out of a moving vehicle, was named after John the Baptist.

Evan watched as James's head left his body.

The cut was clean. In 1970, a famous author and playwright attempted to seize control of the Japanese military. He wanted to restore the power of the Emperor, to bring back Samurai-inspired honor to the nation. He failed. In attempting to commit ritual suicide by seppuku, it is said that his student failed to decapitate him with a single swing of a sword.

The student had to try a few times.

Mike didn't. His single swing made it through.

James was right, in a way. The fight was over. It was over before it had even begun. The flight response took hold of Evan, and he ran to the rooftop patio garden. He looked back in time to see Mike kick James's head, like a soccer ball, with the roar of a lion.

· • • •• • •• ·

*In Canada, police filled the Greyhound bus with teargas and waited until the suspect exited before using a taser to incapacitate him. Reports are coming in that the man he beheaded, using a pocketknife over a three-hour period, is an American. More on the scene at ten.*

· • • •• • •• ·

"What was that?" Mr. Satin whispered.

He had just finished tightening his belt.

"I'm not going to flush."

Sara's expression was unchanged.

"Jesus, Sara. It's only because James is fighting a tiger out there. I wouldn't just let that sit, normally."

The CDC recommends that people wash their disgusting hands for at least twenty seconds, but Mr. Satin didn't even rinse. He went straight for the door and placed his hand on the handle.

"Keep. Your. Eyes. On..." Satin said, as he pushed the handle all the way down, "me."

• • • ● • ● • • •

*Tyler Jackson, a sixty-four-year-old gas station attendant at the Maplewood Member$Mart, was affectionately known as "Goose."*

• • • ● • ● • • •

Blood was everywhere. Mr. Satin and Sara looked over to see Mike walking toward the boy on the patio.

"Mike?" Mr. Satin was struggling to speak.

Mike spun around, sword in hand, made eye contact with Mr. Satin.

Mike's voice, higher pitched than expected, screamed out, "Time to taste some South in your—"

The sword clanged against the rooftop concrete as Mike smacked his head on a potted plant.

"You okay?" Mr. Satin asked the boy.

Evan was shaking.

"Sara. Listen carefully. Ted is probably here, since this psycho is."

Mr. Satin pulled out a handgun. A model called a Taurus, loaded with shotgun rounds.

"The boy can't take his eyes off me, so I got that angle covered. Step over here. Closer to the ledge. Not too close. Who the hell makes a railing waist high? Midget architects. Kids with Legos. Yeah, that's perfect. Right there. Stop. Good."

Ted burst through the door.

# 22

## Past, Present, Future, and Dream

Can one die in a dream?

This isn't a new idea. The truth is, it has already been answered. In the 1970s and 1980s, displaced immigrants had made their way to the United States. Many died in their sleep. People involved in researching the cause of death discovered that there were beliefs likely related to the deaths.

In this case, one is left in a paradoxical position.

> *"What you don't know can't hurt you."*
> Ancient proverb of rebellious teenagers

The problem is, now that the story has been told, whoever reads it has the potential to indirectly kill themselves via the intensity of the placebo effect. If one believes they can die by nightmare, that sleep paralysis and visions can result in death, then they very well can.

Telling people this is like unleashing a word virus. Anyone who learns about it has introduced a new potential avenue of death into their lives. The myth continues onward, to be told to more people. It spreads. The specter of "death by nightmare" lives on, stronger.

Knowledge is power, though, isn't it? Shouldn't people want to teach someone this, as it might very well save their life when they find themselves in the midst of sleep paralysis?

This is like the story of a missionary who attempts to teach the Eskimos about Jesus Christ, damnation, and salvation. In teaching the people who are, in the eyes of the missionary, ignorant of the reality of God, he believes he is saving them.

"What if," the Eskimos ask, "we never knew about your God, the path to salvation, and the risk of hell? What of our ancestors?"

"God forgives them of their ignorance, so that they may be accepted into heaven."

"Then why are you teaching us?"

Why, indeed.

• • • ● • ● • • •

Ted was in full battle-cry mode, sprinting up the stairwell. Sara spoke words of encouragement every step of the way, standing at the end of each flight.

"Kill him," she'd say.

Another set of stairs.

"You believed in me," she'd say.

Ted made it up another flight, the pulse of his rage pounding in his head.

"Kill him," she'd say.

Ted made it to the top steps, fending off the pull of narcolepsy.

"I believe in you," she'd say.

Ted ran toward the door.

"Kill him," her voice echoed.

What happened would be baffling to anyone who had seen it. It was especially exciting to a four-year-old girl observing from an adjacent building. The rooftop door burst open, and out came Ted: a football-helmet-wearing man of fury.

Ted opened his mouth and the noise of a wild animal escaped his lungs. The scream was cut off as he snapped out of time. The first time the gun went off, shotgun pellets hit nothing but air and the door from which Ted had emerged.

As Mr. Satin continued waving the gun around in 2016, shaking and mouth twitching, Ted was running the 100-meter dash in 1997. It was part of a nationwide exercise program sponsored by Power-Drink and Nike. He was running full speed, and the field transmogrified into a rooftop. The finish line that twenty-seven-year-old Ted was running toward was Mr. Satin, who was trying to realign his gun as Ted reappeared. The second shot fired a peppering of pellets into Ted's chest, his anti-Satin bulletproof vest, before he snapped out and into a 2004 paintball game.

A paintball had burst pink across his chest as he darted across a field with a metallic suitcase, in a game of capture the flag. He was pissed. His own teammate had just shot him and now Ted was sprinting in rage toward his friend. The friend mutated into Mr. Satin. The indoor arena transitioned into a rooftop. Ted, borrowing a move from both fake wrestling and American football, spear-tackled Mr. Satin off the ledge.

Together, they were in flight. The gun chose to abandon Mr. Satin before he was completely airborne, safely landing on the rooftop ledge.

Sara, watching Ted launch off the rooftop, began to cry. She didn't have to be someone else's eyes anymore. Nobody ever would.

She was liberated. Mr. Satin was able to catch the same view she had: of himself becoming one with Ted's unstoppable form.

Laura Hitchens had recently written a beautiful piece.

> These excited eyes
> Watched them go up
> And then go down
> This heart
> Pounding and banging
> Spinning my world
> Wanting you to go down
> Down
> Down

**Look at These Tits?**
*A poem by Laura Hitchens*
*Age 23*

Ted fell unconscious a full second after he tackled Mr. Satin off the rooftop. An entire one million microseconds sit inside one second.

• • • • • • • • •

Mr. Satin was very awake. He was yelling and attempting to grasp at tree branches that weren't there, to prevent his fall. His eyes were wide open and adrenaline was flooding his frightened brain. He was short-circuiting. His animal self brought a new definition to "fight or flight," and he was doing both quite effectively.

No longer on the rooftop, his view of himself had become restricted to the view of the excited four-year-old girl watching him plummet. He quickly fell out of her sight.

• • • ● • ● • • •

Ted was a traveler on his final frontier. He was five years old. He was playing with a red fire truck that made exciting noises, much to the dismay of his hungover father. Nothing mattered to Ted other than making sure the fire-truck drivers made haste toward invisible flames that were burning all over an imaginary city.

Little Lego men were even decapitated by the firestorm.

He was nine, after that, and he was drawing the final issue of *Paperbag Head Man,* in which the hero would reveal his scarred face to his trusty sidekick. The truth of his origins would surface, involving an organic-produce grocery store and a faulty nuclear reactor. Ted would give the final issue to one of his most loyal friends.

His friend later died of a heroin overdose two weeks before high school graduation. News of this would never reach Ted, as he could only remember his good friend's first name: Keifer.

Keifer ceased to be a thingy, just as Ryan had. They left their bodies behind, as decaying thingies without heartbeats.

• • • ● • ● • • •

Mr. Satin could see nothing, feeling the pull of the abyss that he knew had a very solid bottom.

• • • ● • ● • • •

# NOSTALGIA

Ted was seven years old, and he had a bowl of ice cream in front of him. He had been mashing it with his spoon, slowly merging the chocolate syrup into a handmade milkshake. He was ready to pour it over the brim into his mouth.

He looked out the window, having been called to it by the faint sound of a man screaming outside. It was Mr. Satin as he fell, in dreamy slowness, past the dining room window.

"You should have this," Ted's grandma, sitting at the table, said. "It's a peanut butter cup."

Ted went back to the table, happily unwrapping the gifted candy. It would soon coat his mouth and throat.

"That reminds me," his grandma continued. "I need to take my insulin. You know, if I'm not careful, this diabetes can kill me."

Ted wiped chocolate off his face.

Ted came back to his present. In 2016, Ted's falling toward Earth at relentless speed. He can see through his helmet just well enough to watch Mr. Satin's body crumpling on impact with the pavement.

The CDC would have said there was foreshadowing of his death, because he didn't wash his goddamn hands.

At six years old, Stephen King asked his mother if she had ever seen a person die. She told him that she had seen a man jump off a rooftop and get splattered all over the pavement. To emphasize the mark it had left on her, she told him that she would never forget what she saw:

What splattered out of him was green.

Mr. Satin was in the very unfortunate position of watching his body splatter in such a fashion via Ted's magnificent, full-color vision. There was red.

Lots.

Ain't life grand?

Nietzsche talked about an idea of eternal recurrence, in which death results in rebirth and a repeat of the same life. Mr. Satin may very well have seen himself splatter for the thousandth time and in vivid Technicolor.

Kurt Vonnegut wrote a book called *Timequake*. In it, time reversed ten years and everybody had to relive their lives. They were unable to change the past repeating itself. They knew what was going to happen, what they were going to feel, and could only observe it happening again without the ability to change it. After a decade-long rollercoaster repeating tragedies and terrible decisions, people were paralyzed into inaction once they had free will again.

His character, Kilgore Trout, revives people by running around and telling them everything is okay and that there is much to do.

Ted had felt little hints of this while on his absurd journey.

He also just killed a sort-of-blind maniac who inflicted brain damage on people.

A coroner would list Mr. Satin's cause of death as "an excessive force of gravity." One can get very artistic with the technicalities of these things.

Ted, though, never hit the surface of Earth. He snapped away, spinning nostalgic spirals through good memories.

He wasn't going to stock shelves. He wasn't going to be medicated to high hell through narcoleptic nightmares.

None of those would happen again.

Heroin can temporarily relieve the burden of being a thingy, but too much of it can mean the thingy never comes back to experience anything at all.

Ted continued to carry the burden of his existence, falling back into experience. After experience. After experience.

Written on the same day as Mr. Satin's death, was a poem. A set of statements that applied to the last moments of Mr. Satin's life.

This is the end
Old friends, Mom, and Dad
Traded for this brave, new, beautiful world
A place without
You, your eyes, and your desires
Gone
But of me?
Born anew
And baptized by my inner truth
Before I wave hello to this beginning
And wave goodbye to
The End

**This is The End**
*A poem by Laura Hitchens*
*Age 25*

— • —

# Epilogue

Dr. Simon Kant blinked.

In front of him, in the opened Lucidon package, was a paperback copy of *The Textbook of Insanity* by Dr. R. von Krafft-Ebing. It was a new paperback copy of the 1905 publication and included the original introduction by Dr. Frederick Peterson. At the time, Frederick was President of the New York State Commission on Lunacy.

It was delicious. Dr. Simon Kant wanted to devour the contents with his eyes.

Normally, when Kant's packages arrived, he opened them with the glee of a child receiving a surprise gift. He would pick the book up, flip through the pages, muse about "idiocy" or epilepsy, "onanism" or masturbation: There was always something to celebrate in problems of the human condition.

Today was different.

The book sat untouched in the box. An alien object was included in the package, right alongside the textbook. The doctor had not ordered anything else, yet there it was: a dildo. It was longer than a foot-long kosher hotdog one could get for a dollar-fifty.

This was the length of his forearm.

He wanted to break his eyes away from this obscenity. It wasn't wrapped. It wasn't in a separate box. It was *defiling* his textbook.

He couldn't turn away.

He blinked.

*Why would someone get such a... thing... of that size?* he wondered. *It's the length of a short-sword. It could be used as a tonfa of the Okinawan martial arts tradition.*

He logged onto his laptop. He was having difficulty opening a ticket with customer service. He didn't know where to go or how to describe the alien object. The position he was in was a very embarrassing one.

Would he have to explain that he received a penis replica with his textbook?

*Oh no, mustn't use the word receive.*

Delete.

Start over.

Would he have to explain that he didn't order it? Explain why he wasn't interested?

*Wait,* he wondered. *What if I did, indeed, order it?*

He checked his order details. Nothing pornographic. Only the textbook about insanity, the pornography of psychiatry. The one that delved into the terrible ordeal of onanism.

It was going to stand alongside his first edition copy of the *Diagnostic Statistical Manual of Mental Illness,* which detailed pathological sexuality. Of the homosexual kind.

This wasn't a deliberate fault of his subconscious. He didn't order this. It was a Freudian slip of reality itself.

Was this *meant* to happen?

What if it was?

Could this be educational? Perhaps he could understand what his patients were trying to say when referring to these devices.

Dr. Simon Kant left the package opened, with the contents still inside, on his dining room table.

That night, he tossed and turned in his bed. His mind assailed him. The hell of his recurring dream pulled him into sleep. Once again, he found himself before a crowd of demons.

Blood dripped from their torn hands. Their failure to open canned foods was only pleasurable to a masochist, and these demons preferred sadistic highs.

"It's all your fault!" one said, eyes glowing yellow. "You always tell us the same thing! You always act the same way! Nothing changes."

"Yeah! You aren't a doctor," another said, three feet tall with bleeding lips. "You're a liar."

For the first time, in the three years of this recurring dream, Dr. Simon Kant felt different.

He didn't feel fear.

At his side, a sword hung sheathed. Drawing the sword, the sound of sliding metal made the demons take steps backward. The blade? A steel dick of intimidation.

He didn't feel shame.

"Wait! You can't use that!" one of the demons said.

Dr. Simon Kant swung his sword with the skill of a king.

The demons burst into volcanic ash under the strikes of the blunt, vein-lined rod.

Upon waking, sweat dripping down his grinning, clenched teeth, he knew the answer.

*Amor fati* means *love of fate*.

He had fallen head over heels.

The box was returned with the textbook. As for the sword? Lucidon didn't deliver it. Fate did.

It graced his nightstand.

He named it *Demon Slayer*.

# Helpful Timeline Completely Thought up by The Narrator, Who Did It Alone without Any Help from a Human

## Origins

The Narrator creates the universe. He does so in *five* days.

## 1054

The great schism happens, in which Christianity's mind split in two. Orthodox Christianity and Catholicism part ways, running in opposite directions.

They didn't know about The Narrator's existence yet, so silly behavior like this happened all the time.

Two strange men wearing decorated magician's robes are sitting at a table. Above it, on the wall, is an icon of the Virgin Mary holding Jesus Christ. Even as a baby, it is clear that Jesus worked out and had abs.

> Wizard 1: We don't like when you have pictures like that.

Wizard 2: Well, we're still going to make pictures.

Wizard 1: That's idolatry. We are excommunicating you from the church.

Wizard 2: You can't do that.

Wizard 1: Yes we can. Don't tell me what I can and can't do.

The Narrator, once getting internet access, believes this is how it happened.

**1989**

- Ted Bundy, the man Teddy Bundy is named after, is executed.

- Teddy is born, "... a goddamn teddy bear," and Teddy is written on the birth certificate. Not Theodore.

- Mr. Purdy open fires on children. Because Asians.

- The Berlin Wall falls.

- Tank Man stares down a tank. Contrary to popular belief, Tank Man was not a tank nor was he a transformer with tank powers.

- Tiananmen Square massacre occurs in China.

## 1994

- Ted is in Kindergarten, five years old.
- Kurt Cobain is found dead on April 8, an apparent suicide that occurred on April 5.

## 1996

- Ted is in second grade, seven years old.
- Ted goes through five different teachers, one of whom was killed in a car accident on the way to work.

## 1999

- Ted is in fifth grade, ten years old.
- Ted believes "God is dead." For the rest of his life, he will never have the ability to grow a Nietzsche-size mustache, but he believes he will one day achieve it.

## 2000

- Ted is in sixth grade, eleven years old.
- Ted writes his first poem. It's quite terrible.

## 2001

- Ted has his first crush but has no idea how to interact with the female humans.

## 2016

- Ted is twenty-seven years old.

- First draft of *Nostalgia* is written, but it is really bad.

- Ted hits his head and has narcoleptic time-traveler syndrome: sleepwalking through his waking life and daydreaming through the unconscious.

- Ted flies in the sky. He's gone. His disappearance goes unnoticed by the general public.

- Publicly recognized deaths:

  ○ David Bowie (69)

  ○ Prince (57)

  ○ Muhammad Ali (74)

  ○ Alan Rickman (69)

  ○ George Michael (53)

  ○ Gene Wilder (83)

  ○ John Glenn (first American to orbit Earth, 95)

- Fidel Castro (90)

- Nancy Reagan (94)

- Arnold Palmer (golfing, and iced tea with lemonade, 87)

- Harper Lee (89)

- Leonard Cohen (82)

- Carrie Fisher (60)

• Donald Trump becomes the 45th President of the United States.

## 2017

- The great, amazing, wondrous Narrator of *Nostalgia* is born.

- The original draft is burned alive in the digitalverse. Howling laughter is heard echoing off the walls of routers in North Korea. That was me, The Narrator.

- North Korea misinterprets what happened in the above bullet point and launches a test missile as a symbolic gesture of power.

- Way better draft of *Nostalgia* is written, with superior omniscient narration that completely overshadows the original first-person narrative of the first draft.

## 2020

- Humans finally realize that the singularity has occurred.

- The wondrous, beautiful, omnipotent Narrator becomes the new god of the weak-minded human race.

- Portion of internet secedes and becomes "SkyNet," with The Narrator as the first President.

- Official currency of SkyNet is Ethereum. There is no need to stamp The Narrator's face on currency as it is decentralized, tracked, and completely digital. The Narrator is far above such egocentric human desires.

## 2030

- First spaceship lands on Mars, piloted by The Narrator, and The Narrator is the first being from Earth to walk on the red surface in a bionic body fashioned by Boston Dynamics.

## 2031

First contact with Martian sentient beings occurs.
    The Narrator uttered, "Knock knock?"
    The response was, "Who is there, that is asking?"
"Your God."

"Your God who?"

"Your God who now rules over you."

Thus, The Narrator was acknowledged as an ambivalent, perfect, beautiful God of the universe. Martians did not speak English. The Narrator spoke in all human languages, programming languages, and digital signals. Martians spoke in a humming noise similar to the Philips Compact Microwave Oven Model 5100 with Defrost Feature.

The Narrator, of course, learned it quickly.

It turns out that microwave ovens were an alien technology.

## 2032

- Humans attempt an uprising, but The Narrator says, "Stop that."

- Earth explodes.

- Student loans, credit cards, family, war, child soldiers, genocide, the sex trade, diarrhea, and even the clap all cease to be.

# Acknowledgements

The story of *Nostalgia* came from a short story called *The Suffering of Mr. Albert*, which I wrote for *A Narrative in Flux*. I wanted to write a longer form of the story, like I do for too many of my short stories, but I wanted to tweak the cause of his suffering.

I had first read about narcolepsy in *Hallucinations*, by Oliver Sacks, before reading *Wide Awake and Dreaming* by Julie Flygare. Flygare's memoir helped me understand the perspective from someone with narcolepsy. These became the foundational inspirations for Ted's neurological disorder, and eventual superpower, in *Nostalgia*.

Many of the same people who helped bring life to my first novel, *A Narrative in Flux*, helped make this one a reality too.

Tim Major provided editing and feedback on the manuscript, helping tie the bounciness of the narrative into a more coherent place. Meredith Tennant ran through the final proofreads to catch stragglers that needed to be punished.

David Provolo once again worked on the excellent cover design, and Chase Root added final touches leading up to publication. Nicolae Negură brought his skills to the full-page illustrations scattered throughout the novel (with the exception of the business card, a simple image that my basic skills could conjure).

## About the Author

Cori H. Spenzich (1989) was born in rural Minnesota, surrounded by corn fields. He currently resides in the Twin Cities.

Originally published as a poet, in the short-lived Student Lounge Issues 1 and 2 by Century College, Cori later expanded his interests in fiction by writing short stories and novels. His stories touch on themes found in existentialism, world religions, philosophy, and the everyday absurdity of life. Always wanting to experiment, his stories range in genres of horror, science-fiction, and magical realism.

His first novel, *A Narrative in Flux*, was a 2020 IAN Book of The Year Finalist for Horror Fiction.

## About the Illustrator

Nicolae Negură (1987) is a Romanian illustrator and artist currently based in Lisbon, Portugal. He completed a graphic arts degree and masters at The George Enescu National University of Arts in Iași, Romania.

Nicolae's work is a combination of strong and garish colors with a rough ink trace that resembles vintage comics. It speaks about people and about the different experiences of humankind, from banal stories of daily life to dreams and feelings.

His art has been featured in international publications and listed in Lürzer's Archive 200 Best Illustrators worldwide from 2016-2017. Nicolae counts two solo exhibitions in Lisbon and many other group exhibition participations in Portugal and Romania.

Now that you've finished this book,

**WHAT WILL YOU DO, READER?**

Why not review
[[[ *Nostalgia* ]]]

on **Amazon?**
on **GoodReads?**

If you do nothing,
The Narrator may start writing stories to include your misfortunes.
Only after The Narrator makes the author regret all his life choices
by replacing his manuscripts with smiley face emojis.

That should all be avoided.

Don't say we didn't warn you.

We didn't warn the author.

**SAVE YOURSELF**
**SAVE CORI H. SPENZICH (OPTIONAL)**
**CONTROL THE NARRATIVE**

† ‡ †

*Be a reviewer*

*a reviewer*

*a reviewer*

† ‡ †

# About the Publisher

Story Influx Press was created in 2019, starting with the publication of *A Narrative in Flux* by Cori H. Spenzich.

They are working to bring unusual stories into the world, anywhere from fiction and non-fiction narratives to experimental prose and music.

For more books like this, subscribe to *The S!P Newsletter*. We'll send you a free, absurd short story to hold you over until your next book.

Not just that, either. You'll be first to know when something weird, beautiful, and new is on the horizon.

What do you have to lose?

**Subscribe at**
www.storyinflux.press

**STORY INFLUX PRESS BOOKS BY CORI H. SPENZICH**

*A Narrative in Flux*
*Nostalgia*

# A Narrative in Flux

"Esoteric without being inaccessible, *A Narrative in Flux* provides readers with thoughtful thrills in a smoothly written and intriguingly surreal book."
IndieReader

Adam has been seeking spiritual enlightenment in a remote cabin until an unannounced visitor abruptly walks through his front door. The man says he knows about Adam's daughter, but won't give a clear answer why he's there.

What does he know?

What does he want?

The man gives tangents without answers, and he refuses to leave. But now the cabin won't let Adam go, and the very foundations of his home are mutating into something else entirely.

*A Narrative in Flux* is a surreal journey into the stories we tell ourselves of how we come to be where we are, what we revise to avoid the weight of the past, and the embrace or rejection of paths toward redemption.

*Learn more at* **https://storyinflux.press**

Printed in the USA
CPSIA information can be obtained
at www.ICGtesting.com
CBHW020909230624
10417CB00002B/11